EXPLORING DARK SHORT FICTION #1: A PRIMER TO STEVE RASNIC TEM

EXPLORING DARK SHORT FICTION #1: A PRIMER TO STEVE RASNIC TEM

EDITED BY ERIC J. GUIGNARD

COMMENTARY BY MICHAEL ARNZEN, PHD

ILLUSTRATIONS BY MICHELLE PREBICH

DARK MOON BOOKS
Los Angeles, California

EXPLORING DARK SHORT FICTION #1: A PRIMER TO STEVE RASNIC TEM
Copyright © 2017 Eric J. Guignard

Edited by Eric J. Guignard
Interior layout by Eric J. Guignard
Cover design by Eric J. Guignard
www.ericjguignard.com

Commentary by Michael Arnzen, PhD
www.gorelets.com

Interior illustrations by Michelle Prebich
www.batinyourbelfry.etsy.com

"Hungry" © 1992 by Steve Rasnic Tem. First published in *Borderlands 3*, edited by Thomas F. Monteleone, Borderlands Press.
"The Last Moments Before Bed" © 2013 by Steve Rasnic Tem. First published in *After Death...*, edited by Eric J. Guignard, Dark Moon Books.
"In These Final Days of Sales" © 2001 by Steve Rasnic Tem. Chapbook, first published by Wormhole Books.
"The Giveaway" © 1981 by Steve Rasnic Tem. First published in *Shadows 4*, edited by Charles L. Grant, Doubleday.
"Rat Catcher" © 1992 by Steve Rasnic Tem. First published in *Dark at Heart*, edited by Karen and Joe R. Lansdale, Dark Harvest.
"The Subject Matter of Horror" © 1992 by Steve Rasnic Tem. First published in *Necrofile #3*, Winter, Necronomicon Press.

First edition published in July, 2017

Library of Congress Cataloging-in-Publication Data
Exploring dark short fiction #1: a primer to Steve Rasnic Tem / Eric J. Guignard.

Library of Congress Control Number: 2017908466

ISBN-13: 978-1-949491-08-1 (hardback)
ISBN-13: 978-0-9988275-2-0 (trade paperback)
ISBN-13: 978-0-9988275-3-7 (e-book)

DARK MOON BOOKS
Los Angeles, California
www.DarkMoonBooks.com

Made in the United States of America

(V052521)

This book is dedicated to those who encourage the written word, those who seek a deeper understanding of literature, and those who simply love dark fiction.

And of course, this is dedicated also to Steve Rasnic Tem, an inspiration to so many. Thank you for consenting to this project.

TABLE OF CONTENTS

INTRODUCTION
BY ERIC J. GUIGNARD

I FIRST READ STEVE RASNIC TEM WHEN I WAS IN high school, about 1993 or '94. The story was "Hungry," included in the anthology *Borderlands 3* from Tom Monteleone. I remember all the stories in that anthology struck me as strange, unsettling things, eye-opening in that they were fantastic and bizarre while still being literary. Steve's stood out, however, not only for its portraiture of sad, poignant family life of an outcast (and also because it involved backstory of carnie sideshows, which particularly enamored me at that time!), but also that the story was honest and heartfelt, even with such an unusual, surreal ending; I "felt" for this impossible character.

It's also the reason I included "Hungry" as the opening story in this mini collection—it was my first introduction to Steve, and so I offer it herein as the same doorway for other readers who may not have yet encountered his work; I happen to like there's a nice synchronicity in that.

After reading "Hungry" I came across an older work of Steve's, "Motherson," included in the 1989 anthology *Masques III* from J.N. Williamson. I don't recall that I entirely understood it at the time, and I loved it for that reason. It's another piece that's amorphous and disquieting, provocative in its portrait of Joel and Samson as they discuss their nameless mothers.

And after "Motherson"? Maybe I'd read next the terrifying "Bodies and Heads" in John Skipp's *Book of the Dead*; maybe it was the weird-though-rewarding "Angel Combs" in 1995's *Year's Best Annual of Fantasy and Horror*; maybe it was the moving "In the Trees," in Stephen Jones' magazine, *Fantasy Tales*. Of course by now I lose count how many stories of Steve's that I've come across in magazines and books ever since those formative days of "adult" teenage reading, though what's never been lost on me is their impact.

See, to put this in perspective, in high school I was in honors English courses, studying tracks on "Women in Victorian Literature" that included such less-than-thrilling fare as *Tess of the d'Urbervilles* and *Madame Bovary* (amongst many, many others of Puritan heroines anchored by the moors of society and class boundaries), while in my free time I was devouring mass market horror paperbacks such as by Stephen King and Dean Koontz. In no way could I ever see the literary integrity of high-minded classics find a middle ground with the mainstream tastes of horror or pulpy genre fiction . . .

Until I read Steve Rasnic Tem.

And that sentiment is only reinforced to me as I now broach my forties and put together this book you hold in hand (or view on-screen). As I review Steve's bibliography—a stupendous 400+ short stories, working with such luminaries as Isaac Asimov, Stan Lee, David Copperfield, et al., not to mention nearly every great fiction publication and editor involved in the last thirty years—I recall the stories I've read and their impression on me. It wouldn't be honest to claim I "like" everything he's written, but nor can I say I've ever been disappointed. Steve always fills his tales with emotion, with imagination, and with significance. The sheer magnitude alone of his output is remarkable; Steve Rasnic Tem's been selling short fiction since about 1976, roughly as long as I've been alive, which to me puts him up somewhere in the stratum between *Inspirer* and *Hero*.

NYT bestselling author Dan Simmons calls Steve "A rare treasure," and author-icon Joe R. Lansdale praises Steve as "A school of writing unto himself." Publishers Weekly has written of Steve, "He has found a perfect balance between the bizarre and the straight-forward," and Library Journal called him "one of the most distinctive voices in imaginative literature."

Steve Rasnic Tem has won the Bram Stoker, International Horror Guild, British Fantasy, and World Fantasy Awards, not to mention the numerous nominations and recommendations he's garnered for nearly every other speculative fiction writing award.

And on top of that, he was kind enough to participate in this project, the first "Primer" I hope to release showcasing diverse modern voices around the world of leading dark fiction short stories.

Following is just an introduction to Steve, and I hope you'll conclude wanting only to search out more.

Midnight cheers,

—Eric J. Guignard
Chino Hills, California
April 22, 2017

STEVE RASNIC TEM:
A BIOGRAPHY

STEVE RASNIC TEM'S COLLABORATIVE NOVELLA with his late wife Melanie Tem, *The Man on the Ceiling*, won the World Fantasy, Bram Stoker, and International Horror Guild awards in 2001. He has also won the Bram Stoker, International Horror Guild, and British Fantasy Awards for his solo work. His novella *In the Lovecraft Museum* (PS Publishing, 2015) was a finalist for the Shirley Jackson Award. His novel *UBO* (Solaris, February 2017) is a dark science fictional tale about violence and its origins, featuring such historical viewpoint characters as Jack the Ripper, Stalin, and Heinrich Himmler. Steve's novel *Blood Kin* (Solaris, March 2014), won the 2014 Bram Stoker Award. His previous novels are *Deadfall Hotel* (Solaris, 2012), *The Man on the Ceiling* (Wizards of the Coast Discoveries, 2008, written with Melanie Tem as an expansion of their novella), *The Book of Days* (Subterranean, 2002), *Daughters* (Grand Central, 2001, also written with Melanie Tem), and *Excavation* (Avon, 1987). A handbook on writing, *Yours to Tell: Dialogues on the Art & Practice of Fiction*, also written with Melanie, appeared in April from Apex Books.

Steve has published over four hundred short stories. His first collection of stories, *Ombres sur la Route*, was published by the French publisher Denoël in 1994. His first English language collection, *City Fishing* (Silver Salamander, 2000) won the International Horror Guild Award. His other story collections are *The Far Side of the Lake* (Ash Tree, 2001), *In Concert* (Centipede, 2010—collaborations with Melanie Tem), *Ugly Behavior* (New Pulp, 2012—noir fiction), *Onion Songs* (Chomu, 2013), *Celestial Inventories* (ChiZine, 2013), *Twember* (NewCon, 2013—science fiction), *Here with the Shadows* (Swan River Press, 2014), and last year's giant 72-story treasury, *Out of the Dark: A Storybook of Horrors*, from Centipede Press, featuring the best of his uncollected horror.

Steve was born in Lee County, Virginia, in the heart of Appalachia. He studied comparative literature and playwriting at Virginia Commonwealth, and received a Bachelor's in English Education from Virginia Polytechnic Institute (VPI). He moved to Colorado in the mid-seventies and received a Master's in Creative Writing from Colorado State University, studying poetry under Bill Tremblay and fiction under Warren Fine. Thereafter he joined the Northern Colorado Writer's Workshop coordinated by Ed Bryant. Over the years the members of this workshop have included Connie Willis, Cynthia Felice, Dan Simmons, Vic Milan, Wil McCarthy, and many other fantasy and science fiction writers. He met his wife Melanie in that workshop and moved to Denver. Melanie passed away in 2015. He currently lives in Centennial, Colorado and has four children and six grandchildren.

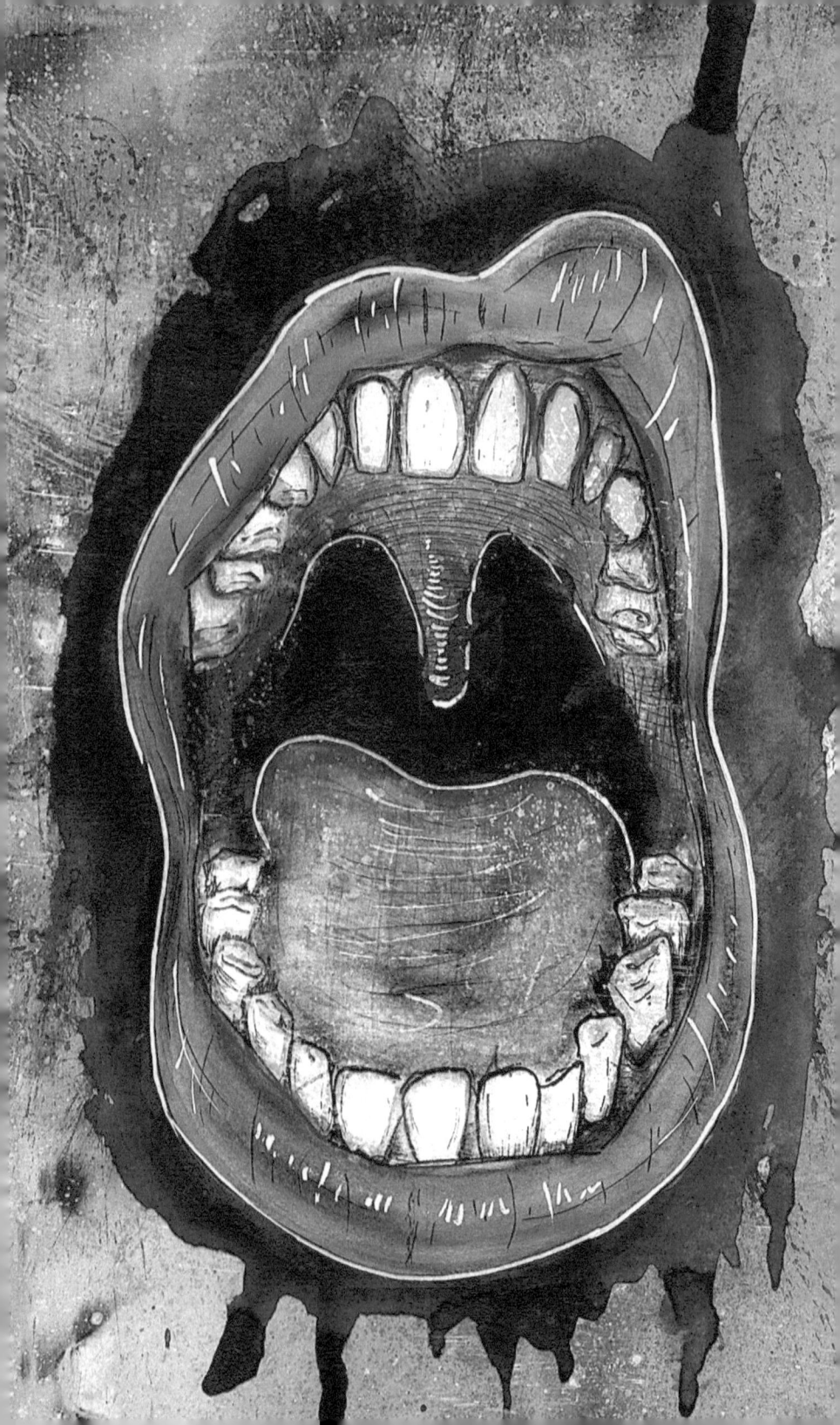

HUNGRY

MAMA?

VIVIAN SPARKS TOOK HER HANDS OUT OF THE soapy water and stared into the frosted kitchen window. There was a face in the ice and fog, but she wasn't sure which of her dead children it was. Amy or Henry, maybe—they'd had the smallest heads, like early potatoes, and about that same color. Those hadn't been their *real* names, of course. Ray always felt it was wrong to name a stillborn, so they didn't get a name writ down on paper, but still she had named every one of them in her heart: Amy, Henry, Becky, Sue Ann, and Patricia, after her mother. Patricia had been the smallest, not even full-made really, like part of her had been left behind in the dark somewhere. Ray had wanted Patricia took right away and buried on the back hill, he'd been so mad about the way she came out. But the midwife had helped Vivian bathe the poor little thing and wrap her up, and she'd looked so much like a dead kitten or a calf that it made it a whole lot worse than the others, so dark and wet and wrinkled that Vivian almost regretted not letting Ray do what he'd wanted.

Mama . . .

But it wasn't the dead ones, not this time. A mother knows the voice of her child, and Vivian Sparks felt ashamed to have denied it. It felt bad, always hearing the dead ones and never expecting the one she'd have given up anything for, no matter what Ray said. Ray wouldn't have let her adopt him, if it hadn't been for those stillborns, but she would have done it on her own if she had to, even if she'd had ten other children to care for. It was her own darling Jimmie Lee out there in the cold foggy morning. It had to be.

Vivian opened the back door and looked out onto the bare dirt yard that led uphill to the lopsided gray barn. Ray's lantern flickered in there where he was checking on the cows. She couldn't see much else because of the dark, and the fog. It was still trying real hard to be Spring here in late March—she'd caught a whiff of lilac breeze yesterday afternoon—but it worried her that the hard frost was going to put an end to that early flowering before she'd see any blossoms. That was always a bad sign when the lilacs came out too soon and the ice killed the hope of them.

"Mama, it's me."

Vivian reached up and touched her throat, trying to help a good swallow along. Suddenly her throat felt as if it were full of food, and she just couldn't get it all down. Ray said it was because of Jimmie Lee, her problem with eating, said it had been like that for her ever since Jimmie Lee came into their lives. "You don't eat right no more. I guess you can't," he said over and over, the way he repeated something to death when he had a mad feeling about it. "Can't say that I even blame you—it's understandable. Watchin' him go at it, it'd put anybody off their food. That's why I never watched."

She guessed there was truth in what he said, but she didn't like to think about it that way. What she liked to think was that it was all her feelings for Jimmie Lee coming up into her throat when she'd looked at him, or now when she thought about him, all the sadness and the love that made it hard for her to breathe, much less eat. And the memory of him touching her on her throat, gazing at her mouth the night before he left home to join that awful show. That was another reason for her to be touching her throat now, in that same place.

"Mama, I come back to visit."

Vivian could hardly speak. Maybe the love in her throat was so big it was closing up her windpipe. "Come on, come . . . on, honey. Been a long time."

Past the east fence she could see the darkness gray a little and move away. She started to walk over but a simple yet awful sound—a young man clearing his throat—stopped her. She clutched the huge lump in her throat. It was warm, as if it might burn her fingers.

"Mama, I ate something off the road a while back. I just gotta get rid of it, then I'll come up where you can see me."

She turned her back to him even though it would have been much too dark to see what he was about to do. But after watching him a thousand times when he was little she felt like he was a grown boy now, and deserved some show of respect, and she wasn't sure but maybe this was one way to do it. At the same time she knew her turning away wasn't all being the good mama, either. She didn't want to see it anymore. She didn't feel like she should have to.

Back in the darkness there was a sound like damp skin stretching, splitting, some awful coughs and gurglings like her son's throat was turning itself inside out (dear God, it's got *worse*!) and then a loud, mushy thump.

A few minutes later she could hear him walking up behind her. "I'm sorry, mama." His voice was hoarse, like he'd been crying. He used to cry all the time when he was little, complaining all the time about being so hungry, and never getting full no matter how much she fed him, how much Ray let her feed him, or however much Jimmie Lee ate on his own to try to fill that awful hunger. His nose would run and his eyes would look all raw and scraped and he'd stop trying to keep himself clean. Vivian took a handkerchief out of her front apron pocket now and turned around to give it to him.

"Thanks, mama. I'll get good and clean for you, just for you."
The young man standing in front of her, saying just what he used
to say to her when he was a little boy and had made himself such
an awful mess, was taller, surely, and had little scraggly patches of
beard here and there where once had been unnaturally pink skin,
but other than that he still seemed the pale, skinny little boy who
had left her years ago. His chin was covered with thick, soupy
slobber which he wiped off with the handkerchief. She didn't
mind—that had always been her job, to provide the handkerchiefs,
the towels, waiting patiently while he cleaned himself up, directing
him now and then to a missed spot or two. Ray had never been
able to stand even that little bit of clean up; he'd always just left the
room.

"My goodness!" She made herself sound impressed, although
what she was really feeling was relieved, and desperate to hug him
to her. "My *handsome* older son."

Jimmie Lee grinned then, showing teeth even worse than she
remembered. She could see that at least he'd been able to get some
dental work done, but it looked like the fillings and braces had
been filed, points added here and there to make him look more
like a silly machine, some big city kitchen gadget of some kind. She
wondered if it really helped him get the food down or if it was all
just for some sideshow or movie work he'd been doing. He'd
written her once about one of the movies—"Flesh Eaters From
Beyond Mars," or some such silliness. He'd said in the letter that
the movie people liked him because he saved them money on
special effects, but she'd never really understood what any of that
was about.

Other than the metal in his mouth her sweet boy hadn't
changed much. Certainly he couldn't weigh much more now than
when he'd left her: his body straight up and down like a sleeve with
no hips or shoulders to speak of, but his neck about twice as wide
as it should be, and faintly ringed, like a snake's belly. Set atop that

stout neck was the largest jaw she'd ever seen—it hung out like the birdbath on top the pedestal she had out in the front flowerbed. His mouth was wider than normal, she guessed, but had never seemed as big as it should be for that size jaw. His lips were almost blue, and cracked, and there were a bunch more splits in the skin at the corners of his mouth. Because of all the stretching his skin had to do there, hair growth had always been spotty. She'd tried to get him to use lotions and oils, but like most children he just forgot all the time. So she'd always rub some into his face every night, being especially careful around the mouth and chin. She wondered if he knew somebody now who cared enough to do that for him.

His eyes were the wide eyes of a lost child's, but then they always had been. Jimmie Lee now was just a larger version of the poor baby that had been born in a backwoods barn and just left there eighteen years before. No one else had wanted the funny looking child but Vivian had known from the very first moment she saw him that this was *her* son, and would be forever. Even Ray, for all his puffin' and embarrassment about the boy, had resented it when one of the neighbors suggested that maybe they shouldn't keep him. This was *his* son, even though sometimes he sorely couldn't stand being around him.

And then Jimmie Lee had gone out into the world, maybe to find his "real" mother, or maybe to find whatever it was he was hungry for. She didn't know, and was afraid then, and was afraid now, to ask. All she'd had to remember him by was this awful swelling in her throat every time she thought of him, and every time she struggled to eat or drink something. But nobody'd ever told her that life was fair to mothers.

"Did you ever find her, son?"

"Who, mama?"

"Why, the one who gave birth to you. The one who just left you here all them years ago." She tried to keep the bitterness out of her voice, but the vein went too wide and deep to hide.

His throat gurgled and a raw smell escaped. She started to turn away, but he held out his hand to stop her. "It's okay, mama. I still got it under control. I'm a lot more careful about how and when I eat now. Something I learned on the road, having to be around other people." He looked at her. She waited. "I never found her, mama. Guess I didn't try much after the beginning. I guess I was a little afraid of what she'd look like."

"You stayin' long?"

"I can't. I finally figured out it's best I be around folks who don't know me so well. But I just had to see you again, and smell you, and listen to you talk. I *had* to."

Her throat filled and she had to force it back down so that she could speak again. "You best get inside now, have something to ... " She looked away from his nervous, hungry face, to where he'd come from in the dark beyond the fence, now turning gray so fast she could see a little bit of what he'd left there: great big mounds of meat still steaming in the cold, their hides partly dissolved away, large hunks of their manes missing, the meat turned to something like jelly, their teeth protruding from lipless mouths. A couple of Winn Gibson's prize mares, she suspected. Well, she guessed Ray was just going to have to deal with Winnie on that one, like he had all those times before. She sighed. "Guess you'd best just get inside ... "

Jimmie Lee held up the brightly-colored, tattered poster beside his face. "It don't look much like me, I reckon, but the owner said they had to exaggerate a little bit to draw a crowd. He said people expected it like that, so that it wasn't lyin' exactly. They called me the Snake Boy." The poster showed a giant snake with her son's lost baby eyes on it, its huge mouth gaped open and an elephant disappearing inside. Lined up into the distance were chickens, bears, and a horse with a huge belly, all with worried looks on their faces.

"That's very nice, son," Vivian said quietly.

"But I only stayed there a few months. I didn't much like people lookin' at me like that, you know, mama?"

"I know, sweetheart."

"It was like the way people used to stare at me around here, only worse. Worse 'cause they were strangers, I guess. I never did like strangers watchin' me while I was eatin'."

"It certainly is impolite," she said. "People shouldn't stare at other people while they're eating. You can hardly digest your food that way." She raised her hand to her throat.

"So that's why I left the show. I did odd jobs after that, until I got to do those movies I wrote you about. And once for a few months I had me a dandy of a job in one of those meatpacking plants. It was late at night, and I had the place all to myself. It was great."

"I'm sure it was, Jimmie Lee."

"But the owner of the sideshow, he really could entertain you. That was a good part of it, mama—it weren't all bad. He'd crack all these jokes when he introduced me, and then he'd make more of 'em while I did my *act*, but all I did was sit up on that stage and eat. But he'd say these things and all the people would laugh and I reckon that's a real good thing. He was real funny, mama, you shoulda seen. You'd a laughed till you cried, I bet."

"I bet I would that, honey."

"We had ourselves enough show 'round here to last us a lifetime, I reckon."

Vivian clutched at her apron. She hadn't heard him come in. She twisted in her chair in time to see Ray throw down his old coat and go stomping off to the bathroom to wash up.

"I guess daddy still don't want me around here." Jimmy Lee sat still with his legs spread, long nervous hands dangling and twisting between his knees.

"Your daddy just gets tired, honey. We all get tired now and then."

She could hear her husband splashing in the water, then hands slapping it onto his face. Jimmie Lee's eyes were large and white in the dimly lit room. When he was small his eyes always looked like that. Before they discovered the hunger he had, Ray used to joke that Jimmie Lee's eyes were bigger than his mouth. "I get tired, too," Jimmie Lee said. "And mama, I still get so hungry."

Vivian couldn't move. She stared at her son with tears in her eyes. "I love you, honey. I just keep loving you and loving you."

"I know, mama. But it's like the love goes inside me and gets lost and then it just isn't there anymore. Like I *eat* the love, mama. And then I'm still hungry."

Ray came back into the room and flopped down into his recliner. He sighed and looked directly at Jimmie Lee. "Well, son, you're lookin'... *better*. Better than the last time I seen you. That's good to see. You doin' a job now? You find yourself somethin' you can do?"

Jimmie Lee leaned forward and tried to smile. But the cracks in his lips and around his mouth bent and twisted the smile. Vivian started crying softly to herself and Ray looked at her with what she thought was an unusual sadness on the face of this man she'd known almost all her life. Then Jimmie Lee must have known something was wrong, because it looked as if he were trying to pull the smile back in, and it just made it worse.

"I left that show, papa. I know that'll please you. Made a couple of movies. And I did some *real* work, too, like at a packing plant, and once I spent almost a year at this junkyard outside Charlotte..."

"Junkyard? You learn the junk business? Now *that* can be a

good trade for a young man. There's *always* goin' to be junk lyin' around."

Jimmie Lee looked down at his feet. "Well, papa, there was pieces the man couldn't sell, and they were just sittin' around his yard, takin' up too much space he said, and he couldn't get rid of them..."

His father interrupted. "You're talkin' about the eatin' now, and I ain't gonna talk about the eatin'."

"But, papa, eatin' metal junk, especially cars, why that's become almost like a regular thing in some places. They put it in the papers, and sometimes it even gets on the T.V. Some fella'll eat a big Buick, or an old Ford Mustang..."

His father leaned forward out of his recliner and stared hard at Jimmie Lee. "We don't talk about the *eatin'* in this house. Look how you've gone and upset your mother."

Vivian sat rock-still in her chair, her eyes closed and mouth open, crying without sound.

"Vivian, why don't you go on out to the hen house and get the boy some fresh eggs? The boy always liked fresh eggs."

She stared at him, her eyes sharp and red. "Wh—what?"

"Papa, I don't need eggs..."

"Sure you do. Vivian, go get the boy some eggs. He used to eat a dozen of 'em at a time, from what I remember. Shell and all. But at least it was real food. Go on now."

Vivian stood stiffly and left the room. She went out through the back door and around the side toward the hen house. But when she passed near the open window of the living room she stopped, because she could hear her husband and her son talking inside. And she knew what they'd be talking about—she knew what Ray would be saying to Jimmie Lee. She crept closer, and stood just under the lilac bush by the window, where she could see their faces, and the feelings painted there.

Ray started talking low and firm. "Now it's good to see you, I mean that, son. I know I ain't always been as soft as I should of when you were at home, but I been thinkin' about you every day since you left us. You been sorely missed—you sure have—and not just by your mama." He leaned back and sighed. "But your mama's sick, boy, real sick, and I just don't know if she can stand watchin' what you go through, havin' it be like it was before."

"Mama? What's wrong with her? Tell me . . ."

"Well, she never did eat all that well, and I reckon we all know the reason for that." Jimmie Lee looked down at his stomach and away. Vivian held her throat and struggled not to make a sound. "But that don't matter so much now. It weakened her, and she's had pneumonia so many times over the years she damn near coughed her lungs out. But she's got the cancer now, and it's clean through her, Doc Jennings says, and she can't have long to go."

Jimmie Lee's face was sheened with sweat. That's what he did, instead of crying. His body never had let him cry.

"Even less, I reckon, if you stay around, son."

Jimmie Lee stood up. "I understand, papa. I appreciate you levelin' with me."

"You're a good son, Jimmie Lee."

Vivian rushed down to the hen house and grabbed what she could, then ran back into the house and into the living room, out of breath, a scarf full of eggs hugged to her bosom. Jimmie Lee was still standing, but had already started for the door. She looked at her husband, then at Jimmie Lee. "You're leavin'," she said flatly. The eggs tumbled out of her arms and splattered across the braided rug.

"I gotta check some things out down at the pasture," his father said, getting up. He pulled on his sweater, started to leave, then walked over to Jimmie Lee and gave him a quick hug.

After her husband left the house Vivian still stood there among the broken eggs, looking at Jimmie Lee as if she were memorizing him, or trying to puzzle him out. Jimmie Lee bent over and started picking up the eggshells. "Leave those alone," she said softly. He straightened back up and looked down at her, his thin lips twitching, the scars around his mouth wrinkling like worms moving across his face. "He told you, didn't he?" she said. "He told you all of it."

Jimmie Lee nodded. "I better go, mama."

"You come here, baby." She held out her arms to him and when he wouldn't come any closer she walked to him and attached her frail body to his. "You're not leavin' me this time."

"Mama, please. I gotta go."

"No, sir."

"Mama, I'm *hungry*." And he tried to push her body away.

She pressed closer, and raised her hand to his lips. "I know, baby." And pulled his thin, cracked lips apart with her fingers. And put her fingers inside her baby's mouth, and then put her hand inside, then both hands. As if out of his control, his huge jaw dislocated, his pliant facial muscles stretched. He tried to pull back, to make his mouth let go of her, but she wouldn't have any of that. "No, child. Just take it, child." His mouth wouldn't let go, and as her head disappeared inside him he heard her say again, "I'm not leaving you."

For the first time in his life, what he ate, all that he ate, became nourishment, and remained inside him.

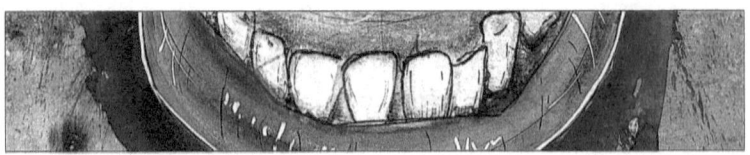

HUNGRY: A COMMENTARY

ONE OF TEM'S MOST UNFORGETTABLE STORIES IS "Hungry"—a Freudian nightmare of epic proportion, told in a tight little tale. The surreal horror of the story portrays a brilliant "reversal" of the mother-son relationship, reframing Oedipal anxiety (not necessarily the infantile sexual longing for mother so much as it is a desire to return to the womb). The maternalistic sacrifice in this story's stunning conclusion is actually a fair trade of a sort, giving the mother what the son once had: bodily union in the belly. The "nourishment" she gives him in her final act is motherly martyrdom—the physical feeding of one human by another—at its most extreme. The "hunger" of the child is absurdly grotesque, an excessive metaphor for the longing one has for maternal sustenance, but in the tale's conclusion, the consumption of the mother is a touching act of love and reunion. What both characters "lack" is fulfilled in the chilling last lines.

—Michael Arnzen, PhD

THE LAST MOMENTS BEFORE BED

"TIME FOR BED, MONKEY," HE WHISPERS TO HIMSELF. His wife used to say that, as did he, when the kids were small. He has not heard that phrase spoken aloud in years.

He examines the six or seven pillows, places them so they will provide support for him in some areas and softness in others. He finds the pillow he will hold tonight, the one meant for his arm, the one he can pretend is close to what he once felt, when she was still alive and this room smelled mostly of her.

If he were more settled, if there were a calmness here, he would have a more exacting routine. Each night the pillows would go into the same positions. It would be the same pillow he would hold. But there is no calm. Each night he must start over, rediscover the geometry that will bring him sleep.

The dog in the corner rises to its feet and looks at him. He cannot see the dog right now, but he can hear it, and this is what it does every night at about this time. He has never been able to see the intelligence in animals that others seem able to see. And he has always been skeptical of testimonies regarding their remarkable sympathy, their unwavering loyalty. But his dog clearly senses something each night at this time. Each night at this time his dog waits as he feels his way through his ritual of arranging comfort, waits until he has turned out the light and laid himself into the hopeful pattern he has made. The last thing he hears each night is the dog dropping its head onto its paws as it finally gives in to its own sleep.

The dog belonged to his wife. He himself has always been terrible with pets. Unfairly, before she died she made him promise he would take good care of this creature. And every day that is exactly what he does.

He always envies the dog because sleep has never come so easily for him. He knows that before this night is over he will have rearranged himself a dozen times in his rehearsals for oblivion, and his bed in the morning will resemble a battlefield.

Years ago he would have spent some moments picturing the locations of his children. He would see them in their beds. He would notice what their little mouths and fingers were doing. As they got older, he would think about them somewhere at the movies, out on a date, and more often than not sleep would have to wait until they came home.

Where were they tonight? Miami, Albuquerque, somewhere in Oregon. Watching over their own children in their beds, wondering about what their own children might be dreaming. Rehearsing, perhaps. Practicing for a life without her, without them. Trying out for the end.

How do you get ready? Can you possibly ever be ready?

One of the last things she ever said to him was, "I'm worried about what you're going to do without me. Your heart breaks so easily, sweetheart."

One of the last things he ever said to her was, "I'll be okay. I have all that scar tissue holding me together."

He reaches for the clock to set the alarm. And stops there, slightly confused. Since his retirement he's never sure what time to choose. He's always tempted to set it later and later, but he worries that late sleeping is a slippery slope—eventually you reach the point that getting up at all appears futile. But shouldn't he be allowed to sleep when it pleases him?

Of course, sleeping has rarely pleased him.

He sets the alarm for ten. He's rarely been able to sleep that late, but it would hardly be a disaster if he gets an earlier start on the day. And if he does manage to sleep until ten he will have just that much more rest, and still be up and alert for lunch.

The final bit of his nightly ritual is to review for himself a mental list of things not done, things not seen, things not said. Did he perform some unasked-for favors this week? He has always believed that life is hard enough—much harder than absolutely necessary—and so we have no business making it harder for each other. He's never thought of himself as a particularly good man, or in any way noble, and the doing of small favors could hardly be called an ambitious undertaking, but at least it is something he knows he can do.

Every week he sends each of his children a letter whose main purpose is to remind them that he loves them. He does not know if this means anything to them now, or if it will mean anything to them later, but at least it is something he can do.

Unable to delay the moment any longer, he lays himself carefully into the arrangement of pillows, pulling on top sheets and blankets as he goes, covering certain areas, leaving other areas uncovered—the same ones each night. When he was a boy he always covered himself completely, cowering there as an aural landscape he dared not picture unfolded around him. Each night he held his breath until he thought his heart would burst and the knowledge that it had not burst the night before still failed to reassure him. Sleep finally came only when he was exhausted and no longer cared whether death decided to take him or not. The next morning was always both bonus and escape.

During the first years of their marriage he could not wait to go to bed. He worked hard at his job, but still found time to socialize, so by the time bedtime arrived he was eager, at times even enthusiastic, for sleep. It was his reward for reaching the end of the day.

As he grew older, digestive problems sometimes made sleep problematic, and during a three year span he slept propped up in bed, fearful that he might drown during the night in his own stomach acid.

These years sleep comes easier again, except for the questions that arrive as soon as his head hits the pillow: *How do you get ready? Can you possibly ever be ready? Will you wake up in the morning? What, after all, have you done?*

He could stay up all night fruitlessly trying to answer these questions, and indeed, sometimes he has, but most nights he is too tired, simply from the prolonged daily struggle with gravity, and so must lie down, must close his eyes, must give himself over to the body's slowing rhythm, to sleep.

Where he goes when the tides of unconsciousness are high enough to cover him is largely undocumented, for he has never been good at remembering dreams, if dreams are what they are. He rarely remembers specifics, but he is often left with a sense the next morning that he had been in the place he should have always been, being the person he was always meant to be. But when he wakes, all he has to show for it is a bitter taste on the tongue.

Tonight his body feels unusually heavy, even though in recent months he has lost weight. When he begins his descent through the surface of the mattress into its interior he isn't in the least surprised, but he is interested. In any case there is no apparent way to reverse the process: the springs grab his fingers, robbing him of leverage.

Out the bottom and through the dust under the bed, then through the floor boards into a maze of pipe and wire, and he closes his already-closed eyes because he is suddenly afraid there may be monsters here, in the dark and under where he has slept his entire adult life. Grown men aren't supposed to be afraid of monsters, but if he has ever been grown he cannot remember exactly when and precisely where it was. He is simply a boy in a bigger size.

This cannot be a dream because he never remembers his dreams, but perhaps the rules are different because this is his last dream.

This fancy makes him afraid again, but he reminds himself he cannot know if this is true. He cannot know if he is alive or dead, sleeping and dreaming, or making some final shift out of the stream of memory and time.

He exits the floor into the wall of the house, then through the brick and then into dark, cold air. Here he sees others much like himself: grown men and women, a few children, flattened thin as paper, floating like leaves, their hands clutching desperately the corners of their new geometry.

Even the birds flying tonight are narrow, and have only one eye. He is sure there will be a number of serious collisions, but they avoid each other without even thinking, though instead of reassuring, this makes him sad. He floats along peacefully and solo, left and right sides rocking gently with the rhythm of his heart.

Far below him a rabbit chases a fox, having a very fine evening.

He thinks about his late wife, and wants to share with her how wonderful it was when that great day came, when all the people at last revealed how they felt about one another, and it was for the first time possible to really see the person speaking inside, without that distracting mask of bruised and twisted flesh they'd all called "body."

But that day hasn't yet occurred . . . Or has it?

He so wants to do a good job. He wants to be ready, but how can you possibly ever be ready for such a thing?

The trees floating by are full of babies, their eyes shining the color of new. He tries to touch one, but navigation is not under his control.

The air is so full of damp only his tears are dry. They make a series of negative spaces on his cheeks, shiny like gems.

How could you ever be ready? The love of his life, had she been ready? Only once did she tell him she was frightened, and it was the worst thing he'd ever heard his whole life. After that she'd told him nothing about what she was going through, just her hopes for the children and her worries for him, and a slow recounting of memories, savoring each one before she allowed it to drop to the floor.

Later (and he had been so shocked by this he could not now remember if it had been three days before her death or three weeks), she had looked up at him and said, "Honey, you know it's not the end of the world."

Just below, barely out of his reach, the world turns over without him. Cows return to the barn, the farmer walking alongside with lantern in hand. A child closes his book, the best he's ever read. A young girl cries herself to sleep, convinced she will never love again. People are dancing. People are making music. People are making love. Their rising voices lift him sideways, almost out of control.

But he knows the world has always moved without him, so how can he complain?

The edges of the sky fray, the clouds grow dirty, and he thinks of a poor woman's dress, and how at the end of a long day of begging she prepares to remove it.

He coughs. He coughs again. A startled head flies out of his mouth. It is his own.

He raises his head and blinks. The numbers on the clock blaze red in the dim landscape of his bedroom, but he cannot quite decipher them. 3 or 4 or 7. Most people die, what do they say, between 2 and 3 a.m.? But still, he cannot read the clock. Zeroes abound. In any case it does not matter. He is alone in his bedroom, in the middle of the night, numbers flashing before his eyes, isolated and lost in the dark. As he has always been. Did she feel this? Was *this* what it was like? He lies down inside the safety of pillows, which can be mountains, which can be clouds, which can be anything he wants them to be. These are the last moments before bedtime, and beyond these walls an eternity waits.

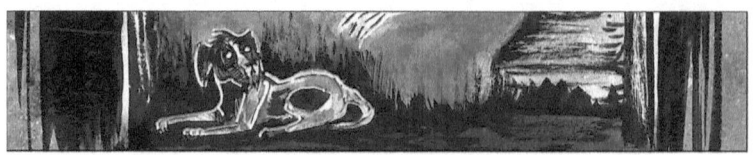

THE LAST MOMENTS
BEFORE BED: A COMMENTARY

ONE CAN'T HELP BUT EMPATHIZE WITH THE
sorrowful widower of Tem's surreal short, "The Last Moments
Before Bed." This contemplative story masterfully builds up our
identification with the insomniac protagonist, a man who we
discover is not only fraught with loneliness in the wake of his
wife's death, but who has been aging and also might very well be
experiencing *the* "last moment" of his life, before resting in peace
under the covers of his death bed.

Or, at least, the protagonist is preparing himself for it. Perhaps
another title for this one would be "Restless in Peace."

Sigmund Freud once wrote about the "Death Drive" and
described it not necessarily as a desire to die, *per se*, but a wish to
die exclusively on our own terms, in a manner of our own
choosing. It is a wish for the ultimate control over the unknown—
and a dream which is impossible, ultimately, to achieve, because

the reaper always has his hands on the handle of the scythe, not us. When I read the surreal journey that the protagonist of this story endures, I am reminded of this compulsion. And perhaps the "fantasy" in this story is the extreme empathy the protagonist expresses at length—which is itself a way to die "happily ever after" with his wife. In that way, it is a love story—and a tale of rescue.

What makes the story ingenious is that not only does Tem blur the boundary lines between the world of dream and that of reality, but also suggests that the world of dream is also a kind of afterlife, in itself.

—Michael Arnzen, PhD

In These Final
Days of Sales

MAIN THING IS, YOU'RE SELLING SOMETHING THOSE
folks need, something they can't live without.

"It's not the bang in your buck, it's the buck in your bang." At
the end of the commercial the words blaze a brilliant white across
the black screen, then fade. Emil remembers a time when clarity
was of the utmost importance in sales, conventional wisdom being
that people would not buy an unknown quantity. Of course, what
they thought they were getting might not bear much resemblance
to the object eventually delivered wrapped in brown paper
C.O.D., but at least the transaction began with that image in
mind, clear if erroneous.

Now, a certain degree of clairvoyance is required to discern
what goods are actually being advertised. Emil, himself in the sales
business, watches commercials in the hotel rooms along his route,
trying to map out exactly what the rules are now. What troubles
him most is that they seem to be not just about new sales
techniques, but about a change in the human psyche itself. We
have become the creatures in our dreams, he thinks, poured into
pleasing and biodegradable packaging.

People want something—that has been the message behind
the message in every ad or commercial. *You want something*, they

remind us. The ads advertise *want*. They advertise *need*. No wonder the actual product remains in the background. At some level the advertisers have finally realized their products are merely symbolic, almost irrelevant.

Much of the mysterious advertising, Emil has finally concluded, is for various brands of pants.

After a few years, all the towns, all the countless burgs and villes line up like endless doors opening one by one, and seem like the same town, the same Main Street with the same row of worn brick or white-washed wood on each side, the same people of pink or yellow or brown in their denims, corduroys, cottons, or polyesters, waving or not waving depending on how friendly toward strangers they are feeling on this particular day. And yet Emil, the professional salesman, has never really thought of himself as a stranger.

That was the first thing he learned in sales: you cannot act like or think of yourself as a stranger. Not if they are going to trust you. Not if they are going to *buy*. And how is buying any different from shaking a hand, giving a good how-do-you-do, getting married, kissing the kids good night? Not much, when you really think about it. Just another form of social exchange, value for value, you rub my back and I'll rub yours. You don't want to be left back on the shelf when everybody's buying. That's the very worst thing. You don't want to remain unsold all your life.

Sometimes Emil is so intent he is on the eventual accounting that he forgets sales is more than that. It is a matter of wishes and dreams, of planning and foresight, of frustration and expectation. After years on the road, each town is exactly what he'd expected it to be. The streets are exactly what he'd imagined; the people are perfectly familiar because they've already walked these streets in one of his countless motel daydreams.

It is as if, every day, the citizens of these tiny communities rebuild their town according to his expectations, anticipating his particular arrival. Given how self-centered human beings are, this is no doubt a common misperception. It is one of the first things you learn as a salesman, and if you are good at your job, you use it to your advantage.

Emil is not good at his job. In fact, if there is a worse salesman out there on the road Emil has not yet met him. The man with the off-kilter eyes fills the screen with a loopy grin. A dolly back to reveal the rest of the family: the wife rubbing up against him in her new red dress, barely able to contain herself, the kids jumpy. Emil thinks the boy may have peed his pants.

They are all holding up great wads of fake cash to the camera; the portrait on one of the bills resembles Clark Gable more than any president Emil can think of. And yet these people are so thrilled to have it in their hands—they jump around as if affected by some nervous disease.

Having little tolerance anymore for the manic patter of commercials he keeps the volume down as he watches the television family pantomime surprise, joy, delirium. They've gotten what they've always wanted, or at least now they can afford to buy what they've always wanted. Failing that, perhaps they can rent it. If it's still available. If they can ever figure out what it is.

He really shouldn't make fun, he thinks. If people didn't behave this way, if they stopped looking for something to make them happy, they wouldn't buy.

Of course, people seldom buy from him in any case. In fact, Emil has come to think of himself as the Anti-salesman, like some super villain with a huge gray cape and unpleasant teeth.

Emil has in his pocket a letter from an old salesman he used to meet out on the road a couple of times a year. Their paths might cross in Goodland, or in Hugo, perhaps even in Kansas City. Supposedly Walt had been quite successful in his time, but Emil knows him only as this tired-looking fellow who might have been a retired teacher or someone recently recovered from a lengthy illness.

"Emil, this is a job offer of sorts. Not for a specific job really but it is the promise of a job, a good job with regular hours and good benefits. And there's *no* travel involved. My friends and I have had this dream we've developed over years on the road, a dream built a stick at a time in hotel rooms and all night diners, of someday having our own town, a factory outlet town where customers would come to *you* to buy the things they really needed to buy. So no sales pitches or how-many-should-I-put-you-down-fors. Why, any pressure high or low would simply be out of the question! We need salesmen to run the stores of this new town, trained salesmen who have become more interested in helping people than they are in earning high commissions . . . "

Emil has taken this letter out and unfolded it and reread it so many times it threatens to fragment into a dozen or so worn paper squares held together by a few commas and dashes.

He has never visited this new town. It just makes him feel good knowing that it is there.

Sometimes Emil fantasizes that he will find a way to sneak back and catch the residents of a town unawares. Then he will find out exactly what each of these places is really like. Perhaps at last he will discover what people really think about him. The thought is both exciting, and dreadful.

Emil's career in sales hasn't always been like this. In the beginning he never knew what to expect when he arrived in a new town. It had been interesting. It had made him anxious. He never knew if he'd find hell or a paradise. Most of the time it had been neither, of course, a necklace of gray towns and gray people, but at least that heady anticipation had always been there.

"The *main* thing is..." Jack looked around for a place to spit. Emil moved his feet out of the way. Finally the old man looked over his shoulder and spat behind him. "Main thing is, you're selling something those folks *need*, something they can't live without."

"I don't want to lie to anybody," Emil had said.

"Lie? Who said anything about lying, boy? I don't want you to *lie*, for chrissake! Who knows what anybody needs? I don't know what you need. Are you arrogant enough to tell me you know what *I* need? Do you really know what *you* need? I doubt it. Even occasional self knowledge is a rare thing, boy. It's luck, pure and simple. So don't talk to me about lies. Guesses, would be more accurate."

"I don't even know what I'm selling," Emil said.

"That's because I haven't told you yet, boy." Jack pulled an oft-creased, yellowing square of paper out of his back pants pocket. Ignoring the tiny paper slivers that flaked off and littered the floor, he unfolded it, unfolded it again. When it was about a yard square he stopped and pressed his nose against it. The paper was so worn and discolored it made Emil think of a thin layer of old skin. He could practically read Jack's expression through the huge square: the wrinkled forehead, the pursed lips, the mushy dark gray eyes like a baby's. But Emil couldn't make out any of the writing, or even if there was any writing.

"There's some difference of opinion on this." Jack's voice raised and lifted the paper as if it were a floating tissue. "But encyclopedias best for a beginner, I suspect. You're offering them the world of knowledge, the flying carpet to distant lands, all of that for just a few bucks a month. Just gotta remember that with encyclopedias you only call on people who have kids."

"Because most adults think their learning days are over," Emil added helpfully.

"Somethin' like that. Tell me, are *you* willing to learn, or do you just want to put your own two cents in?"

"Oh, yes, I want to learn. Really." It was just to be a short term job following graduation, something to put food in his mouth and a roof over his head until something better came along.

"Okay, then. The thing about selling encyclopedias is you can convince them they need to buy a set for their kids' futures. Everybody wants to do things for the future of their kids—in this country we spoil them rotten."

Emil's own parents had begrudged him every penny. You would have thought they might have found the cure for cancer if only they hadn't had to worry about their only son.

If he ever had children, if he ever could convince a woman he was worth raising a family with, he'd surely buy them a set of encyclopedias. A whole damn library. You could not do enough for your kids.

"You'd buy your own kids encyclopedias, wouldn't you? I mean if you had any?" It was as if the old man read his mind. A good salesman, according to that first training manual, could tell when interest had peaked, when the customer was growing bored, as well as determine the particular magic phrase that might turn sales, and lives, around.

"Oh, well, of course. If I had the money . . . "

"Even if you didn't have the money you'd do it! You'd find a way somehow. Now don't tell me that you wouldn't!"

"Well, you're right . . . "

"See now, *that's* what I'm talking about. In this country we buy our kids things, especially if we have even the vaguest notion it'll give them a better life than what we've had. Something bright and shiny, and fluttering with color and motion. That's pretty much the American way."

Jack somehow found an opportunity to drop the word American into practically every conversation, his particular style of sales patter. Emil wasn't sure he himself had his own style, even after all these years, except that it involved a great deal of sitting, of daydreaming through visits in old-fashioned parlors and newly-decorated living rooms, waiting for a change in the air or the light, or the order of the universe.

"You know, I've never sold anything before," Emil said.

"Sure you have. Like everybody else you've been selling all your life. The question is whether you've been giving the people good value."

Sales had been as unlikely an occupation for someone of Emil's temperament as anything he might imagine. He'd gone on very few dates, unable to sell himself to women. He'd been passed over for the simplest jobs, because he'd been unable to sell himself to employers. Whatever friends he had acquired seemed largely accidental.

He had no aptitude for closing the deal, shaking the hand, laughing at the obligatory jokes. It was the world's sense of humor that had brought him into sales after graduation—you understood that sort of thing if you were a salesman.

So it had all come down to the day he'd picked up his sample set at the warehouse, along with the brochures and studies proving how kids raised on encyclopedias had increased IQ, appetite and stamina, and set out his first time on the road using the route map the old man had given him. Instead of the usual dots or squares to represent towns and cities, there were little drawings of houses, all of them the same size, crude yet childishly cheerful, pastel yellows and blues and pinks. When he examined those tiny houses with his magnifying glass he spied children's faces in the windows of several, here and there a smiling mother or father out on the lawn, baby brother in a stroller, the shirtless neighbor watering his lawn. A tiny blotch of ink that might have been a dog, or a cat.

A company-owned car was provided for his first trip out. Imagine, a company car! But he was alarmed to discover a broad scrape along the length of the passenger side, and cracks in the windows. "They want you to keep that passenger side parked away from your customers' houses at all times," the chief dispatcher informed him.

The brown dashboard had enough cracks in it to fill a dried-out riverbed. The clock was missing an hour hand (if he scrunched sideways against the steering wheel he could just see that missing hand reclining in the bottom scoop of the dial). The seat and back had even more cracks, futilely repaired with a variety of tapes that caught and pulled at his neatly pressed suit.

Out on the road he realized that major cities—New York, St. Louis, Philadelphia, Chicago—weren't even depicted on the map. "We like to leave the big places for the veterans," Jack had told him.

Now and then over the years he would come to a town that felt far more familiar than most. With a "B" name like Bennett or Bailey or Baxter, it would be a town with ambition: the main street in the process of restoration, new motels and restaurants at the outskirts, and at least one new mall. A construction sign just outside town limits advertises a multiplex. Overpriced town homes are being erected along the distant foothills.

Emil has met the desk clerk at the cheapest hotel and asks about the health of his youngest daughter. The clerk does not act surprised. At the bake sale outside the post office, the woman in the bright yellow dress sells him a small bag of ginger snaps for the eighth time this year.

In the windows of the hardware store are pictures of missing children. It is an epidemic; he wonders about the strangers who steal children out of the Baileys and Baxters and Bennetts of the world. Perhaps the kidnapper is an airline pilot, he thinks. Perhaps he is the representative of some obscure government regulatory agency. Perhaps he is a travelling salesman who is lost in the identical towns and quiet streets of America.

It never occurs to him, that anyone might suspect him, anymore than it would occur to him to commit such a crime.

The automobile on the flickering screen is unlike any Emil has ever seen: so sleek, so modern, it appears to drive itself, passing without damage through tornadoes, mudslides, nuclear attacks. The message of the commercial is that a person could not die in such a vehicle. Death has always been the big mistake, the nasty trick, the unacceptable penalty. Emil believes if he just didn't have to die he might someday become a successful human being.

Now, in these final days of salesmanship, Emil is on his twenty-sixth company car. He knows this from the files of paperwork in a cardboard box in the back seat. He wonders if bad driving is one of the by-products of salesmanship, this pushing through the highways and byways of the assigned route, whatever the weather or road conditions, this nervous and careless passing, this incessant hurry to get nowhere. If it all came down to driving habits, he'd have been declared the perfect salesperson a long time ago.

But he has no talent for sales. He sometimes wonders what kind of man he must be, to spend his life dedicated to something he is so poor at. But if he has learned anything at all in his wanderings it is that life itself, for most of humanity, is this constant doing and undoing, doing poorly at what we attempt, undoing the better efforts of those who have come before us.

Still, survival requires food for the mouth, a pillow for the head, motion of the eye and a new day's list of prospects for the brain to process.

In these last few days of salesmanship his lack of aptitude cannot be helped. In these last few days of salesmanship there are many more towns to investigate, hotel rooms to rent, long hours to spend waiting on the couches and good chairs in the living rooms of America, meditating through the afternoons in quiet contemplation of the people who need everything and nothing. He means no criticism in this, it is simply the life we live in these last days of sales, trying not to think too much about the small tragedies or joys.

The sound at the door is more a rubbing or a scraping than a knocking. He hesitates to open it—no one knows he is here except the clerk.

A small old lady of gray flesh peers up at him beyond the dire weight of her glasses. "I just wanted to thank you for that new Bible you sold me," she tells him, and lifts her head to kiss him on the cheek, exposing the ragged hole in her throat.

He tries to close the door on her, but she shoves the shiny red leather Bible between the door and the jamb. He turns to escape and trips over his sample case. She drapes herself over him, whispering, *I just want you to sell me again,* and he is appalled to discover the erection growing like an impending purchase beneath his belt.

Remember that there's a pit waiting for you in self pity, so put that I in try and get back on your feet and run!
The cheers, the applause, the feet stampings are so loud Emil is compelled to fiddle with the volume control. It takes some time for him to figure out that the dark-haired man on the screen is not a preacher, but a salesman like himself. Or not like himself, for this man is wildly successful the world over.

The man sells tapes and books, and a correspondence course of some sort, but even more clever than that, Emil suddenly realizes, the man is *selling people back to themselves.* An incredible idea—an endless supply of product with so little overhead.

There is a sadness about it all, he thinks, but who is he to say? Who is he to even have an opinion on such matters?

That A in ambition is as high as any mountain, but climb it anyway! Don't eat the pear in despair. Remember there's no hope in dope! Take that H out of whining and you'll be winning!

Emil cannot understand why the company has never fired him. In all his years on the road he has never once met his quota. And yet he has been allowed to continue making contacts, meeting prospects, conversing for long, leisurely days in the living rooms and on the front porches of America.

Periodically the home office sends out trainers (usually men) whose job is to sharpen the skills of the sales force. He isn't sure what their real job is—half the time they make no pretense of training.

Just as he suspects, their courtships of his customers are for the most part rewarded. It is amazing, sometimes frightening, to watch as the salesman nods, and the customers nod in return, as smile echoes smile, and laughter echoes laughter, as the customers slowly transform into salesman doppelgängers, and a good time is had by all, except for Emil, who stands by the door and attempts to shake off his anxiety.

Many of the salesmen appear to achieve their success by means of sheer animal dominance. These are the alpha males, and although the herd of customers may mimic the salesman's gestures to the point of slavishness, they can never hope to match the salesman in strength or confidence.

Other salesmen at first glance appear to be no more impressive than Emil, but they are persistent almost to the point of their, and Emil's, humiliation. He spends one appalling afternoon camped out on a front porch, the fox-like salesman with the wired eyes refusing to leave until the elderly couple has purchased something. The husband gives in with shaking hands and cornered eyes.

A few of the men the company sends are interrogators, and they grill many of his prospects as to their needs and dreams, why they were at all hesitant to buy such a fine product. They use the customers' own hesitations and rationalizations against them.

And there are those for whom Emil can think of no better word than crazed, the ones who affect a certain delirium—dancing a jig, forcing facial spasms, singing spontaneously and inappropriately—that so troubles the customers they buy what they can in order to get rid of them.

Emil, of course, is unlike any of these salespeople. There is no good reason for the company to retain him, and yet he remains year after year, hoping for the blessed dismissal which will free him, which he cannot ask for himself, and which never comes.

And here he is again, the wife on the couch making polite conversation, the husband puttering around in the next room, pretending to make repairs, but whose real business is to listen in on the wife's dealings and make sure she does not spend too much of their rapidly disappearing funds. The wife has no real desire to buy except out of politeness or pity. Her real need is to have someone to talk to about the children, share her memories of the sister's dead baby, her own medical troubles, her thinly disguised fears that her world is a precarious thing about to end, and her husband will not listen, has not really listened in years.

Outside it is a kind of Kansas, although they are miles and years from that state: sun burning the distant edges of crops, the horse moving slowly across the hill, the small boy on his bicycle struggling through mud ruts deep enough to swallow his wheels.

Soon the wife will offer her final apologies, so many unexpected expenses of late, folks hereabouts having pretty hard times, such a good product it's really too bad we don't have the money to spare, I'm afraid we can't see our way and it's not your fault at all ...

And he will happily be free once again to step outside and stride to his car, relieved that he will not have to fill out all the paperwork that an actual sale entails.

"So my husband agrees we should take one, at that discount rate you said you were offering today, one time only and not to be repeated and who could pass up such a bargain, I mean, *really*."

Emil stares at the young wife as if she has suddenly gone crazy, as if she's been spitting and drooling and speaking in tongues. But in fact she is an older woman, graying at the temples and wearing an old fashioned housecoat fading into transparency around the hem. He cannot understand—it is as if he's nodded off with the unending familiarity of his own sales spiel, and the woman's mother has replaced her in the chair. He gazes around the vaguely familiar room and sees her elderly husband slumped forward in his overstuffed chair, sleeping or dead.

"Just a minute," he finally manages to say through a rising panic, "Just a goddamn minute!" Has he really cursed a customer? "I've got my order book here somewhere. We'll get you fixed right up. Yes, indeed, you won't be sorry about *this* purchase, *nomaam*! It's the gift that keeps on giving, the key to a lifetime of success, the satisfaction of knowing you're doing... you're doing, well, what you're doing, it's the cap ... on the toothpaste, the bridge ... "

Emil's hand flops about in the worn out leather satchel like a broken sparrow. He's not sure what he's seeking, in fact cannot remember the last time he'd reached into his sales valise, when his fingers seize the tattered edges of the sales book and retrieve it carefully as if it were some moth losing wing scales in frightening amounts. He spreads it open on his lap, carefully positioning the disintegrating slip of carbon paper, writes "1" as the quantity, then stops.

What is he selling this woman? He looks up at her expectantly. "You wanted one ... " His dry tongue adheres to his bottom lip.

She smiles so broadly he thinks her mind is, in fact, gone, and he will not have to complete the order form after all. But then she nods slowly, happily, as if perfectly aware that she is doing the right thing for herself and the generations to come.

For the briefest of seconds he is unable to pull his tongue from his lip, and when finally he does it is so painful he feels a tear balanced dangerously in the corner of one eye. "One ... " he repeats, and looks around for the sample he has been showing her, but it is nowhere to be seen.

"Deluxe edition," she finally replies, so he knows it isn't the Sports Weathervane, or the Speedo pocket groomer, or five of the twelve handy household helpers he sells, or used to sell. If he could only remember what it was he was selling this trip out, what he had put into his sample case, but there is nothing there, and nothing anywhere to be seen but this giant book bound in red leather she grasps so lovingly in her two, trembling hands.

"I only wish our son Johnny would read this with us. So long he has been away from the Lord . . . "

"One Deluxe Bible, Red Leather, with the special painted map inserts tracing Jesus's path through our mortal world," Emil says confidently, writing *1 RB* onto the pad.

He settles back, calmed, as the elderly woman (but he recognizes her now, remembering how he had stopped here when she *was* a young bride, and realizes how much she must regret not having bought that Bible the first time he came by, when her baby was still a magical creature of hope and possibility) drones on about the sorry affairs of her son, the all too familiar litany of failures and small betrayals.

Gazing out the window Emil sees a small blond boy on a backyard swing, perhaps this woman's grandchild, or impossibly, her son at a better age, conjured up by her sad monologue. Emil rises from the chair—the woman does not seem to care, or notice, while the husband continues his uninterrupted rehearsal for death—and climbs out the window, strides across the bright lawn bordered in corn and sits in the child's other swing, the one reserved for playmates yet to arrive.

"It's too nice a day to be indoors," he says, both an explanation and an introduction.

"Who are you?" the little boy asks, staring up at Emil's face.

Emil gazes out over the endless and precisely aligned rows of corn. The sun glazes the leaves a green-gold, and he feels a smile travel unbidden across his face. "I'm nobody, really," he finally replies. "Just a salesman, calling on your parents with my promises and offers, my bag full of hope and secrets."

Suddenly stern, the boy says in an old man's querulous voice, "Are you going to try and sell me something?"

Emil is startled. He has been asked the question before, and it never fails to upset him. "No, no," the salesman in him lies. "I'm not selling anything today."

"Then what are you doing here?"

"I'm spending time here in this swing. I'm the customer this afternoon, buying myself a piece of this beautiful day."

The boy stares intently over the corn as if seeing a body hanging from the line of the horizon. When he looks back at Emil, his expression is eager. "So you've been to a lot of different places, not just here?"

"More places than I can count, son. I hope you don't mind the familiar."

"And the people in these places, they're all different in these places?"

"Well, you know it's funny that you should ask that, young man. It's been my experience that people are the same the world over, subject to the same wants and needs, accessible by the same techniques."

"No, you're lying!" the boy shouts. "Tell me that they're *different*! They *have* to be different from here!"

"Well . . . " Emil scrambles for the right words that will calm the boy, that will sell him some peaceful behavior. "We wouldn't understand each other too well, now would we, if we were all that different from each other."

"Get off my swing!" Alarmed, Emil trips getting out of the swing and sprawls on the ground. He heads back toward the open window, dusting off his pants as he goes. Behind him the boy sobs, but Emil will not let himself turn around. Customers don't like it when you watch them cry.

He climbs back through the window and slips into the chair. Spying a strand of burry weed stuck to one dress sock, he leans forward to remove it. The woman continues narrating her list of sadnesses. But it is not the same woman. This woman is younger, a brunette, and although the room is of the same style as the previous one, there are differences.

This husband is livelier than the other one. He rushes back and forth, a gun in his hand. "You hear that?"

After some delay Emil realizes the question is addressed to him. And then he *does* hear something coming from outside: gunshots and shouting, the alarmed cries of animals.

"What..."

"It's that Wilkins boy—Johnny! He shot his ma and pa, and now he's killing all the livestock in sight!"

Emil can hear a rumbling engine between the shotgun blasts. "But he's just a boy..."

"Sixteen if he's a day! Old enough to blow a stranger's head off if he's dumb enough to stick his head outside! Guess he didn't read those encyclopedias you sold them ten years ago."

Crazily, Emil wonders if the Wilkinses had purchased their easy annual update volume subscription plan. It has been designed to keep your youngster apprised of all the latest developments not only in the sciences but in the arts as well.

An hour later it is all over. Emil cannot remember if this family has placed an order or not. But there is such a relief in leaving a customer's house he could care less. It is the best he ever feels.

Emil comes out of the house feeling that now would be a good time to take a walk, a relaxed stroll through a friendly neighborhood where he has lived all his married life. Their kids know his kids—they don't always get along but they play together every day—and he sees the parents at the grocery, in church, and every other Wednesday night for bowling. They aren't exactly friends, but there is a kind of comfort in these small, recurrent encounters. It is a good life, if you avoid looking too many steps ahead.

When he sees his battered black Buick parked at the curb, he recalls that he is a salesman, has never been married, and has very few friends to speak of. His key sticks and hangs, as if the lock mechanism has not been used in some time. He is careful not to strain the key too far as he manipulates it against the roughness of the internal workings, and finally there is a giving, and a surprised suction as he jerks open the door.

Inside, the air is as thick and cloying as the air trapped in a dead grandmother's old trunk, and the fast food wrappers layering the floor appear to have been there for years. He sits in a bed of dust as soft and thick as another layer of upholstery.

He has no hope of starting this vehicle. This is a dead machine, designed for the transportation of the dead. He puts his key into the ignition and turns it anyway. There are no signs of electrical activity. He gets out of the car and looks under the hood. The engine appears to have been ripped out ages ago.

When he calls the main office he is too embarrassed to tell them that the car is an ancient piece of junk which has not been driven in years, because of course this would make no sense. He simply reports that his career in sales has outlived another vehicle, and that he will need a replacement. They authorize a budget and he picks a used car dealer at random from the phone book, his only criterion that it is within walking distance.

He waits at a safe distance from the car lot and watches as people drive in, are greeted in rapid succession by eager, excited salespeople, are spirited away to the cars that will change their lives, the cars that were made for them and them alone, with bucket seats, SRS brakes, extras and more than extras, the cars that will strain their marriages and bankrupt them. Many of these customers already know the possible end result of their reasonable time payment purchases, are perhaps even determined that it not happen to them again, and yet they will be so excited, so agitated by the experience and all the grand possibilities they will be absolutely thrilled to pay more and more for less and less.

Emil has an advantage. For so many of these people, a new car means a new life, transportation out of bad decisions and past mistakes. For him it is simply a continuation of the long, sad trip he has been on all of his life.

He waits until the right couple comes in driving the roughest, most battered vehicle he has seen in years. But it does not smoke, and there is no obvious wobble as it pulls in front of the dealership. An hour later they drive away in a bright blue teardrop of promise, and he walks across the street and into the sales office.

"What do you mean that doesn't include floor mats?" speaks a surprised voice out of a tiny office to his left.

"I want to buy that car, there," Emil says to the first salesman to approach him.

"Excuse me, sir?" Emil might have asked to buy a tombstone in a shoe shop.

"That car, there."

The salesman glances over Emil's shoulder without much interest. "Must be a trade-in. It hasn't been worked up yet."

Emil struggles to look the man directly in the eyes. "That's the one I want."

The salesman attempts to stare him down in the friendliest possible way. "What if I told you I could get you into a better car for less money?"

"You and I both know how much it's worth," Emil says a little shakily. "Take that figure and add fifteen percent." He forces himself to pause, and looks even more directly at the man. He isn't

sure if he's pulled off a smile. "I'm a salesman, too. Since college—
it's the only job I've ever had."

The car salesman nods, unimpressed, and Emil decides this has
been a failure. "I'll have to take this to my manager," the salesman
says, and for an unreal moment Emil thinks he is about to be
arrested. Emil gazes after the man as he enters another office, waits
anxiously as the salesman confers unemotionally with his boss who
glances up at Emil only once, then down at a notepad. The boss
gives the salesman a piece of paper, who carries it out to Emil and
puts it into his hand. He almost expects the car to stall out as he
drives it out of the lot, which would be embarrassing but survivable.

Studying the violent screen flickers of these motel room TVs,
Emil has developed a theory that these sporadic discharges of light
are part of an attempt to hypnotize the viewer into buying
whatever product is being discussed. This sales maneuver is doubly
clever because these residents are generally poor travelers who
cannot afford to leave their rooms. They watch these commercials
in a state of desperate exhaustion.

A collage of images impresses onto the tired and ill-used tissue
of his brain: children, small tidy houses, walks in the park with the
family dog, vacations at the beach. *Be A Man* floats eerily across
the screen in colors muted to suggest a whisper. *What are they
selling?* There is no way to determine. Whatever it is, it is certainly
something he does not have.

ARE YOU READY? in bolder than bold type shouts at him
from the screen. He waits for the kicker, the product revelation,

the final sales pitch before he is returned to their regularly scheduled program. But there is no return. There is no change. The words remain frozen, oppressive, unforgiving, even when he unplugs the television in frustration.

Emil is travelling I-70 just outside Salinas when he sees the billboard "The City of Commerce" with a huge red arrow perched on top. The sign is somewhat worn, but he thinks maybe this is from the road construction he's seen in the area over the past year. He thinks of the letter folded up in his pocket, and he turns onto the access road: all black and shiny with promise.

He might quit his job this very day, call the company office and have them pick up the car and his samples if they care to bother.

He passes no cars on the road and considers the afternoon heat and thinks this must be a slow time for shopping traffic. He spies the gleaming steel tower from a couple of miles away, a variety of buildings spread about its base like flowers planted around an airport control tower. In the afternoon sun everything gleams like a nest of needles. Just before he turns onto the main street, another large sign appears. *Welcome to the City of Commerce*, with a picture of a happy little girl gesturing to the wonders behind her. *Alice in Wonderland*, he thinks, and the artist's vision of the shopping centre confirms the notion—it might easily grace the cover of some edition of something by Carroll or Baum.

Emil is bewildered by the cold tears he feels leaking from his eyes. What is happening to him? He should just turn around. "City of Commerce" indeed. It almost makes him laugh.

Then he sees the bullet holes above the little girl's head almost making a halo, the torn passages through the faded backdrop of city.

A turn onto the main street of the City of Commerce confirms that the place has been abandoned for some time. The finished buildings appear empty and the unfinished buildings ready to collapse beneath their architecturally unsound frameworks. He has nothing better to do—never did have—so he continues his leisurely drive past the vast fields of asphalt.

The streets appear to have been laid out with remarkable care: a perfect grid of block after block of abandoned buildings, partially finished constructions, lots full of dried up landscaping, mounds of mysterious concrete, in one place a huge outdoor skating rink (*Remarkable! Ice skating in Kansas!* The signs scream.) Now it looks like a large, shallow swimming pool with no water, much less ice. Remarkable, indeed.

The abandoned construction sites in particular draw Emil's eye. Much of the time he cannot tell what the building was intended to be. Multiple girders jut out sideways in parallel like huge claws taking a swipe at the sky. Rooflines twist and turn like the skeletons of roller coasters. Giant square passages where walls might have been form windows for watching the world change color. Enormous Mondrian sculptures line up like a fleet of cubist spaceships.

He parks along one street of gravel and sand and peers through the great transparent teeth of a clownish building with round window eyes. The swirling pink and orange paint job within makes him think of an ill child after a day's overeating at the circus.

What might they sell in such places?

The fact that the buildings are relatively new, unlike those in the Western ghost towns of old, fills him with a peculiar dissonance, as if he is hearing dozens of ill tuned chimes playing nearby.

He turns the corner and is face-to-knee with a silver metal beaver at least a dozen feet tall. Beside it, and still gigantic at half the beaver's size is a brilliant white fiberglass baseball. The beaver's eyes are wide and staring, as if it is as surprised to see this baseball as Emil is.

He can find no specific business these statues might be attached to and therefore assumes this must be some sort of installation of public art. He wonders about what the customers must have thought of these two objects, forever how long this place had customers.

As he walks past the rows of storefronts it occurs to him how insubstantial everything seems—the empty stores like huge display boxes having no value without their goods. The wind thunders against the expanse of glass and shiny metal. There are no indications of residences, of schools, or any other structure where the day-in and day-out of life might take place. But of course, this is the City of Commerce, a container for commercials and impulsive retail exchange. Now even the signs indicating what might have gone on here are gone.

One door is slightly ajar. Emil tugs it lightly and slips inside. This one has been occupied at one time—the outlines of counters and shelving decorate the floor. Dead electrical cables dangle where light fixtures have been removed. Here and there lie a candy wrapper or a bit of a magazine, gray tracks in the dust where small creatures have roamed. There has been surprisingly little vandalism.

"You don't belong here." The dry voice speaks from behind.

Emil turns to see a man with one hand poised over a holster. "Hey, easy now," Emil says softly. "I . . . I have an invitation, I guess, to work here." He slides one finger into his front pants pocket, fishing for the paper, careful to let the guard see the rest of the hand. He retrieves the letter and extends it.

The guard shakes his head. "Not necessary—I didn't think

you were the stealing type anyway. You're the salesman type. I've
seen a lot of you around here, sniffing around. All of them had
letters like yours."

Emil puts the paper back into his pocket. "What's to steal
around here anyway?"

The guard looks around the vast room as if for the first time.
"Fixtures," he says, with a hint of sadness.

Emil walks past the guard and out the door. Then he pauses.
"How long?"

"Oh, about three years."

"What happened?"

The guard smiles a little. "They had a huge supply of what
people didn't want."

On the otherwise unnaturally quiet walk back to his car, Emil
finds himself chuckling aloud.

In these last few days of sales, generous discounts can be
offered, bonus gifts pulled out of the dusty trunk and placed into
hesitant buyers' hands. In these last few days of sales, he is full of
compliments and important news for everyone's family. In these
last few days of sales, he represents the church, the school, and a
benevolent government. In these last few days of sales, he cannot
remember what he is selling, nor does he recognize the odd objects
in his sample case. In these last few days of sales, he cannot bring
himself to ask *Which do you like best?* and *How many should I put
you down for?* In these last few days of sales, he knows that
sometimes a customer just wants a warm body to talk to. In these
last few days of sales, he sees all the lonely people on his list, all the
sad people for whom his brief visit is a major event.

He has been travelling for quite a long time. *Of course,* he thinks. *You're a career salesman—you've been travelling forever.* Towns have died during the time he has been a salesman. Local economies have been disrupted. Great masses of people have lost their definition, reduced to reading self help volumes and watching far too many movies. Everyone he meets is desperate to sell, but so many are reluctant to buy, having been disappointed so many times, having been cheated and lied to, having been murdered for their dreams and ambitions.

The towns he passes through are painted in FOR SALE signs. People have moved on ahead of him. Those left behind in the streets walk aimlessly with eyes like dull pennies.

In these last few days of sales, he yearns to complete one last transaction. Coming upon the white-haired man out on the street thrills him as nothing has in years. He lets the man have one last swig from his bottle, then props him against the wall. The old man resembles Jack, the fellow who trained him years ago, but he resembles the guard at the City of Commerce as well. He may resemble the salesmen who built the City of Commerce, but Emil doesn't know how they might have aged. He resembles most old men Emil has ever known. Perhaps he resembles Emil himself, who has not looked at his own face for a long time.

"You only want the best for them," he begins. "Your children. Your grandchildren. And if you don't have children it's the children of others you want to thrive—is this not so? Because then you can believe that something of this life will go on, and do well, and make of itself a thing of beauty against the failing of the light. For what else is there, but the spark of us carried by children into the lands where we will never travel?

"And so you buy them things, grand things your own parents

could never afford. And you hand these things to them, as if you were handing down sacrifices and offerings to some fierce and unstoppable god. 'Take these things I have given you and do well,' you say. 'Make my dreams into something capable of movement and breath. And do not damage me, make no attempt to rob me of my last remaining dignities because I swear, I only wish you well.'

"And that's the best you can do. That's the best any of us can do, in these final days of sales."

Placing his sample case on the concrete in front of the old man, he goes into the trunk of his car and hauls out box after box of Bibles and encyclopedias, grand dictionaries full of ideas he has never been able to express, baskets of outdated kitchen accessories which have lost both their utility and their names, perfumes and cleansers, small gifts for every occasion. The old man stares drunkenly at the salesman, unable to manage even a thank you.

The salesman walks away empty handed, leaving all the voices, all the give and take and the I've-got-something-special-for-yous behind, knowing full well that he will not have to sell himself to the rain, or the wind, or the ground with its daily increase in gravity. And there is a peace in knowing that not all deals have to be closed.

From the outside, his home looks no different from all the others. This is the way he wants it—there is a comfort in the cloning of every house he has ever seen on television, the slavish duplication of columns and brickwork, the same angled roofs repeated again and again across the horizon to become a geometry of reassurance.

Emil has no reason to leave his house. The company pension provides for him quite comfortably. Why he should be receiving a pension, why they should reward decades of poor salesmanship, he has no idea. But then reward and punishment has always been a puzzle he is unable to solve.

Groceries can be delivered relatively cheaply from the smaller stores. Items may be ordered over the phone even without a catalogue: he will work from lists of merchandise but pictures of anything are forbidden in his house. He receives a daily newspaper, but pays the man next door a handsome sum to censor it for him, until the paper is like lace in his hands, beautiful in its way as shreds of celebrities and the dire news of the world allow the morning sunlight to pass through, making intricate shadowscapes on his Formica kitchen table.

He spends much of his day walking around naked. He has grown increasingly uncomfortable with clothing: even the plainest garment seems to evoke one style or another, and then he feels he is wearing packaging, and cannot breathe until it is shed.

Without clothes he can clearly see the damage that wraps him. There are cracks in his lower face and left arm from hours driving directly into the sun. There is dry and flaky skin across a chest and abdomen which no one has touched in years. There is an arthritic right hand which burns and freezes in the position of one asking for money. Several of his toes are missing. He does not remember what he did with them.

He has lost the full range of motion in his left arm. His left leg twists awkwardly inward, making it painful to maneuver up and down steps. *I didn't even sell these things,* he thinks. *I was never that good. My arms, my legs, my hands, my heart pulled and squeezed: I just gave them all away.*

His front doorbell rings. He peers out a nearby window. A small boy, staggering under the weight of a large box, looking up at Emil's closed door forlornly, as if behind it lies the only safety the boy has ever known, and yet the door must seem hundreds of miles away. Emil wraps a towel around himself and goes to greet his visitor.

The boy's eyes grow huge when he sees Emil. But he musters his courage. "Sir, I'm trying to earn extra money this summer selling these fine candies . . . "

"Son." Emil crouches next to the boy, careful not to expose himself. People are scared, they're scared everywhere he's ever been, and he doesn't want them to get the wrong idea. "Son, listen. You've got to get my *attention* first. Then you've got to pique my *interest*."

"Peek, sir?"

"Then you have to show me some *conviction*. Then you have to kindle my *desire*. And finally you have to *close* the deal. Nothing really happened here today if you can't manage that last part. It was all just a dream, one big fantasy if there's no closing. AICDC, son. Attention, interest, conviction, desire, close. Remember that."

Emil realizes the boy is staring at his belly. Poor salesmanship, drawing the prospect's attention to his own faults. "So are you gonna buy a candy bar, Mister?"

"Say I do buy a candy bar from you. What are you going to do with the money? Are you going to save that money, son?"

"I'm gonna go to the movies with it, if you buy a box of 'em. Six to a box. Ten dollars."

"Okay, then. I'll buy two boxes."

"Do you have a wallet, sir?" the boy asks skeptically.

"I own a wallet, even a pocket in a pair of pants to keep it in. I probably even sold myself that pair of pants. I don't always walk around naked, you know?" The boy continues to stare at him. Emil stares back. Finally Emil asks, "Do I give you the money first, or do you give me the candy bars first? Anymore I'm not so good . . . at this commerce thing."

When they find him a week later only half the candy bars have been consumed. The property is on the market for several years before it finally sells, longer than any listing the local realtors can remember. In fact, the poorly painted "For Sale" sign becomes a familiar landmark that the neighbors actually miss when it is gone.

In These Final Days
of Sales: A Commentary

THIS BRAM STOKER AWARD-WINNING NOVELLA IS a slow burn surrealist tragedy that depicts both a dying industry and dying worker in that industry—an average salesman careening toward the end of his world of endless pitches and personal failures, and the end of meaning that such a world itself inevitably falls prey to. It is also an example of Tem at his most literary and difficult. The horror here is far more existential than many genre readers might expect.

The salesman in this story is both a victim of the world of advertising and a perpetrator of it by virtue not of skill or even active agency, but through passive reproduction of its ideology. He is like a cog in a larger machine of consumer capitalism that is falling apart. Though Tem's surreal approach persistently resists easy explanation, this story's fantasy functions most overtly like a "dreamwork Marxism," as the narrative critiques the failures of rhetoric and consumerism to contribute to human society (and therefore, survival). Emil, the protagonist, is a kind of alienated laborer in a job that isn't really labor at all, so much as rhetoric—the job of manufacturing need and making a sale. The problem is that there are no more boundaries between home and work life for this zombie of marketplace reality. The final town that he winds up settling for is a world of emptiness, where the only hope he has is to pass along what he has learned to a new generation, giving himself away at a dirt-cheap price. Tem hints that this is a kind of abstract retirement village for salesmen, so the ending is fitting. But the emotional arc of this story lands in one place, and it is not a pot of gold at the end of any proverbial rainbow: in retirement, his only hope is to reproduce the system by passing down his empty knowledge to an echo chamber of a world where "products are merely symbolic, almost irrelevant."

—Michael Arnzen, PhD

THE GIVEAWAY

"Be good, sweet maid—"

"IF YOU DON'T CUT THAT OUT, SOMETHING REAL bad's gonna happen to you!"

Six-year-old Marsha dropped the second handful of mud she was about to smear on seven-year-old Alice Kennedy's party dress. "Like what?"

Alice made a thinking face for a little while. "Well . . . I might tell your daddy about it and he just might give *you* away!"

"*Nu-uh*," Marsha grunted. She proceeded to gather another handful of mud. Some of it splattered onto her shoes and she had to twist each foot just so to wipe them in the grass. It was hard to do that and still hold onto the slippery mud. Then she walked carefully over to where Alice was sitting making mud pies and raised both hands.

"Stop it, Marsha! I told you what I'd do! I'll *tell* and he'll just give you away!"

Marsha didn't understand why Alice didn't want her to smear mud on the dress anyway; it was nice and cool and besides, Alice's dress was already muddy from making mud pies all afternoon. But she was even more confused about this 'giveaway' stuff. She'd never heard of that before.

"What do you mean, give me away?"

"I'll tell him you've been real bad to me, Marsha, and he'll give you away to some other family, or even worse!"

Marsha just looked at her in confusion. "Moms and dads don't give their kids away," she said seriously.

Alice looked up from her mud pie and smiled. "That's what your daddy did with your brother, Billy."

"That's not true, Alice Kennedy. Billy died and went to heaven!"

"How do you know? Did you see him go?"

"Well, no. But Daddy told me he did."

"They *have* to say that, stupid! They don't want you crying and making trouble."

"Don't call me stupid!" Marsha watched her shoes squishing into the mud. "Why did they give Billy away?" she asked softly.

"I heard your daddy tell my daddy that Billy was too small and that he'd never be very big, ever. He sounded real sad about that. So I guess he just gave him away so he can get a bigger boy later on."

Marsha nodded solemnly.

"Know who else got given away?"

"Who?"

"Johnny Parker."

"I 'member him! He was like a grownup 'cept he had something funny-wrong with his head made him want to play with kids all the time. But he went to a special school. My aunt said so, and she's a teacher!"

"Well, he was gonna go to one of them schools, but they gave him away instead. Know who else?"

"Uh-uh."

"Shelly Cox. She kept breaking things and being mad and real mean, and one night her daddy had them take her away."

"Who's them?"

Alice looked back over her shoulder at the backyard of her house. "I don't know for *sure*. Guess who else?"

"Who?"

"*You*, Marsha, 'cause you got my party dress *all* muddy and my daddy's probably gonna want to give *me* away, so I'm gonna have to tell on *you*."

"Tattletale!" Marsha cried, tears streaming down her face.

"Crybaby!" Alice yelled, running toward her house.

Marsha threw a handful of mud after her in frustration. "*Nu-uh*," she grunted as she began the long walk home.

There were loud voices coming from the kitchen when Marsha got home. She could hear her mother crying, her father shouting. He sounded real mad. Marsha hated it when they had a fight. She sat down in a chair in the living room, picked up one of her books, and pretended to read. But she could only pretend because they were too loud.

"Can't you do anything so simple as enter a check properly, Jennie? I bet Marsha could do that and she's only six years old!"

"I'm sorry, Ted. I just forgot! Will you leave me alone?"

"If I let you alone we'd be broke within the month! Last week you took out the grocery money twice and caused six checks to bounce! And you *say* you don't know what happened to the money! You're driving me crazy, Jennie! I can't take it! I tell you I can't take it anymore!"

"I've *tried* to be a good wife to you . . . " Her mom started to cry and cough, and Marsha couldn't tell what she said anymore. She wanted to go in and see her mom, but she was too afraid. Her daddy was shouting louder than ever now.

"You haven't *been* a wife to me, since Billy's been gone!"

Her mom was crying louder than before. Marsha could hardly understand her. "The doctor says . . . you know the doctor said I can't have *any more*!"

"You're lying, Jennie, you're lying through your teeth. I know that quack's nurse! You've been lying to me, lying all the time. You just *don't want to,* Jennie. *You just don't want* to!"

Marsha went upstairs until dinner. She thought her daddy noticed the dried mud on her shoes when she got up from the table, but he didn't say anything.

Marsha woke up with it still dark outside. Something told her she should go to the window. She was afraid, because it was real dark out there, but she thought she should probably go. She tiptoed as softly as she could, afraid she might wake up her dad.

A funny-looking car was parked in front of the house. It was long and black, the longest and blackest car she'd ever seen. And there was a long silver thing, jagged like lightning, that went from one end of the car to the other. This lightning was brighter than the streetlights and hurt her eyes.

The car windows were gray. They looked dirty. She couldn't see through them at all.

Marsha didn't want to see the big black car anymore, but she was more afraid not to see it. She didn't know why she was more afraid of not seeing it, but she was.

Marsha tiptoed down the stairs in her pajamas, scared to death that her father would catch her and maybe give her away like he had Billy. She went into the dark living room. The front door was wide open; she could see the long black car by standing in front of the open door.

She stepped carefully onto the front sidewalk and started walking to the car. She tried to be as quiet as a mouse like her aunt had told her once. She was scared of the car, but she had to keep walking toward it. She couldn't understand that at all.

When she got to the side of the car she held her hands up to her eyes and leaned against the window, trying to see what was inside. But it was too gray, too dirty, too dark. She started to walk around the front of the car and to the other side to look in the windows there, when the tall man stepped in front of her.

He was tall with black shadows all over him, and he had a big white bow tie and a big white flower on his chest, but she couldn't see his coat, he was so black, so she didn't know how the flower stayed on.

The tall man bent over. He had no face, just a head full of white fog, like his face hadn't made itself yet.

Marsha began to cry in a soft voice, scared to death she'd wake up her daddy and he'd give her away for spoiling his sleep. But she couldn't help crying, and it kept getting louder and louder until she was suddenly wet and warm and she knew she'd had an accident and he'd want to give her away for that too.

She turned around to run back into the house.

Two men with no faces stood there, carrying a long thing between them. Marsha was so surprised she stopped crying.

For some reason she wasn't so afraid now, so she walked up to the long thing they were carrying to see what it was.

Her mommy was tied to the thing and she was looking up with her eyes all funny and her mouth open and oh she knew her mommy was dead, oh *dead dead dead*!

She ran screaming into the house, and they grabbed her, and she was screaming and they put something into her mouth—

Only "they" was her daddy. He was sitting on the sofa now, looking all serious like when she'd done something real bad.

"You saw the car?"

She nodded tearfully.

"Your mommy went away in the car?"

"Ye—es," her voice broke and she cried a little.

"Okay, I want you to listen, Marsha." He held her chin up and made her look into his eyes. "Your mommy didn't do things right, Marsha; she wasn't *good* enough. So you know what happened?"

She nodded solemnly. "I . . . think so."

"I had to *give* your mommy *away*. That's what happens to people who mess up. You've got to do your *best*, do your best for *me, all the time.*"

Again she nodded, but then her father was gone, as quickly as he had arrived, and she was alone on the couch in the darkened living room. She looked out the window but nothing was there. She knew everything was all over, then.

Marsha sleepily climbed off the sofa and stumbled around trying to find a light switch. She couldn't find one so she had to make her way to the kitchen in the dark. She would have cried then, but she really didn't feel like crying anymore.

The kitchen light switch was too high, so she had to work in the dark. It was hard to find the pans or the turner in the dark, but she finally did. At least the refrigerator light let her see the eggs, and she kept the door open afterward so she could see better.

She knew she'd better start her daddy's breakfast now if she was going to get it finished on time. The stove and counters were real high for her, so it would take a long time.

Daddy liked big breakfasts, and more than anything else in the whole wide world, she wanted to please her daddy.

THE GIVEAWAY:
A COMMENTARY

"THE GIVEAWAY" IS A CLEVERLY PLOTTED STORY ABOUT a simple fear: abandonment anxiety. Children perhaps do fear that their parents might "give them away"—trading them in to make space for a better child if they don't behave, as Alice Kennedy teasingly suggests to Marsha in this creepy work of flash fiction.

But on a deeper level, Tem unveils how fear is a weapon, used to enforce a gendered power relationship. The twist ending here results in a mother, not a child, being taken away (or murdered—the difference is blurrily irrelevant in the story), and thereby compelling Marsha to make pancakes for daddy in the end as a means of surviving a potential repetition of his wrath. Fear is used to keep Martha in her place as a woman—not only "to please her daddy"— but to *take the place* of her own mother.

This masterful story shows Tem at his most feminist, giving us an allegory about compulsory motherhood, women's "duty" in the domestic home, and the unfair patterns of patriarchal rule.

—Michael Arnzen, PhD

RAT CATCHER

JIMMY HADN'T CAUGHT FOUR HOURS SLEEP ALL week. Normally he was a dead man about five seconds after he hit the sheets. In fact he liked telling people, "I work like a bastard for my sleep eye." Not that he didn't lie there staring at the ceiling a few hours now and then, but not like this, not for days, not for a week. Sometimes he might lie awake counting the tiles because he was trying to remember something, even though he might not know he was trying to remember something. Some special butt-saving part of his brain would nag at him until he'd think of that anniversary, birthday, or special favor for his boss that he'd completely forgotten. "Ah, Jimmy, thank you," he'd say when he remembered these things, flat on his back in bed. Sometimes Tess would nudge him with her elbow a little when this happened, pretending to be asleep but still letting him know he'd saved his butt by just a hair this time (she figured he'd forgotten something having to do with her and most of the time she was right).

But not this time. He didn't think his lack of sleep had anything to do with her. Not this time. What he forgot this time, he knew, came from somewhere deeper than that, from somewhere further back, off where the dog bled in the dark and the rats gathered round to lick the blood.

"Ah, Jimmy, thank you . . ." he said, but quietly, not wanting Tess to hear. *Off where the dog bled in the dark . . .*

Maybe he felt the scratching before he actually heard it. Later he'd wonder about that. He felt it up in his scalp, long and hard like fingernails scratching through a wooden door, the fingers bleeding from the effort and the mind spinning dizzy from the pain. Jimmy raised his head and looked toward the bedroom door—they always kept it open halfway and the hall light on because Miranda was just down the hall and at five years old she still *hated* the dark, almost as bad as Jimmy used to hate the dark. Almost as bad as he hated it now. They kept the door open because Jimmy wanted to be sure and hear her when she screamed, which she still did about once every two weeks. He didn't want to lose any time getting into his little girl's room.

Tess was always telling him that he coddled the kids. That was a funny word—he didn't think he'd ever heard anyone else use it besides his grandma, back when he was a kid. And maybe Tess was right. He'd never been able to talk much about what it is you do with kids—being a dad to them, disciplining them, that kind of thing—not the way Tess could. Sometimes she gave him these books to read, books on parenting by experts. He never got much out of them.

All Jimmy knew was to pay attention to them, love and protect them. And tell them when they did wrong, though after a while you couldn't stop them from doing wrong, just slow them down a little. Just doing that much wasn't easy, not like it sounded. The kids would find out soon enough that the world was worse than they'd ever imagined, and maybe they'd hate him a little at first because of that. But all he could do was try to keep them alive and teach them a few things that would help them keep themselves alive. And maybe someday they'd figure out he'd loved them and that he'd meant the best for them, even with all the mistakes he'd made. He figured love was mostly mistakes that turned out okay. And maybe he'd get lucky. Maybe he wouldn't be dead when that someday came around.

A small black dog, maybe a cat, came racing by the open door, in and out of the little bit of light like a shadow pulled by a rubber band. On its way to Miranda's room, looked like. But they didn't own a dog, not since they put old Wooly to sleep. And their cat was white as a clean pillowcase.

Kids scream for all kinds of reasons. But even for the silly ones Jimmy had never been able to stand it. When Miranda's scream tore so ragged out of the dark he was up and heading out the door without even pulling down the covers. Tess made a little gasp of surprise behind him as the headboard rocked back and banged the wall. The whole house was shaking with his legs pounding down the hallway and Miranda screaming.

As soon as he reached his little girl's door he caught the sharp smell of pee, and when he slammed the light switch on he fully expected to find the rat up on the bed with her, marking her with his teeth and claws and marking the bed with his pee just to let Jimmy know whose was whose. But there was just Miranda huddled by herself, her face red as a beet (how do little kids make their faces go that color?), and the damp a gray flower opening up all around her tiny behind.

"Daddy! A big mousy! Big mousy!" she screamed, words he would have expected from her two years ago but not now (Dad! I'm a *big* girl now!), pointing a whole pudgy and shaking fist toward her open closet door. Jimmy ran back into the hallway and Miranda started screaming again; he could hear the baby squalling in the back room and Tess and Robert were out in the hall, Tess shouting, *What's wrong!*, but Jimmy could hardly hear her over Miranda's *Daddy!* He waved a hand at Tess trying to get her to stay back, jerked open the hall closet door and grabbed the heavy broom, and ran back into his daughter's room.

Where he slammed her closet door as far back as it would go and held the broom up, waiting.

Miranda's screams had choked off into hard, snotty breathing. He could feel Tess and Robert behind him at the door, Tess no doubt holding Robert's jaw in that way she had when she wanted him to know he shouldn't talk just now. Daddy's real busy.

Suddenly there was movement at the bottom of the closet: Miss Raggedy Ella fell over and Jimmy could see that half her face had been torn away into clouds of cotton and he just started whaling away with the broom on Miss Ella and Barbie and Tiny Tears and Homer Hippo and the whole happy-go-lucky bunch until they were all dancing up and down and laughing with those big wide permanent grins painted on their faces (except for Miss Ella, who now had no mouth to speak of) and screaming just like Miranda did. "Daddy, stop! You're hurting them!"

"It's a rat! A rat, goddamit it!" He didn't know who he was yelling at; he just didn't know how they could be bothering him when there were rats in the house.

Eventually he stopped and when there wasn't any more movement he used the straw end of the broom to pull out Miranda's toys from the bottom of the closet one by one until it was empty.

He found a flap of loose wallpaper along the back wall above the yellowed baseboard. He lifted the flap up with the broom handle and discovered a four-inch hole in the plaster and lathe.

It took Miranda a long time to go back to sleep that night. She was trying to forget something but that part of her brain expert at saving your butt wasn't letting her forget so easily. Instead Jimmy knew that memory was getting filed back there where the rats lick the blood off the wounded dog.

Tess kept telling him, "It's all over now. Go to sleep, honey." And finally he pretended he had.

And thought about the rats he didn't want to think about living in his house, sniffing around his kids. He wasn't about to forget that one. He wasn't about to forget any of it.

He'd never thought that his momma had a dirty house, and he didn't think the other ladies in the neighborhood thought so either else they wouldn't have kept coming over to the house, drinking coffee, eating little cakes his momma made and getting icing all over the Bicycle cards they played with. But this was Kentucky and it was pretty wet country up their valley down the ridge from the mines and half the rooms in that big old house they didn't use except for storage, and fully two-thirds of all those dressers his momma kept around were full of stuff—clothing, old letters, picture albums, bedding—and were never opened. His momma never threw away anything, especially if it came down from "the family," and she had taken charge of all of grandma's old stuff, who had never thrown away anything in her life either.

So it was that he found the nest of hairless little baby rats in that dresser drawer one day. He wasn't supposed to be messing with that dresser anyway. His momma would have switched him skinny if she'd have caught him in one of her dressers.

Back then they'd looked like nasty little miniature piglets to him, squirming and squealing for their momma's hairy rat-tit, but not quite real-looking, more like puppets, a dirty old man hiding inside the dresser making them squirm with transparent fishing line. He'd slammed the drawer shut right away and good thing, too, because if he hadn't then maybe that dirty old man would have reached his burnt arm out of the drawer and pulled him in. Jimmy's momma had never told him to be scared of rats but she sure as hell had told him all about the ragged, dirty old men who stayed down by the tracks and prowled the streets at night looking for young boys to steal.

He never told his momma about the rats either and they just seemed to grow right along with him, hiding in their secret places inside his momma's house. Like the rats he'd heard about up in the mines that grew big as beavers because they could hide there where nobody bothered them. He'd heard that sometimes the miners would even share their lunches with them. Then the summer he was twelve the rats seemed to be everywhere, in all the closets in

the house and you could hear them in the ceilings and inside the
floors running back and forth between the support beams under
your feet and his momma got pretty much beside herself. He'd
hear her crying in her bed at night sounding like his dear sweet
little Miranda now.

He remembered feeling so bad because he was the man of the
house, had been since he was a baby in fact and he knew he was
supposed to do something about the rats but at twelve years old he
didn't know what.

Then one day this big rat that should have been a raccoon or a
beaver it was so big—a *mine* rat, he just knew it—came out from
behind the refrigerator (that always felt so warm on the outside,
smelling like hot insulation, perfect for a rat house) and ran
around the kitchen while they were eating, its gray snake tail
making all these S's and question marks on the marbled linoleum
behind it. Jimmy's momma had screamed, "Do something!" and
he had—he picked up the thick old broom and chased it, and that
big hairy thing ran right up her leg and she screamed and peed all
over herself and it dropped like she'd hit it and Jimmy broke the
broom over it, but it started running again and he chased it down
the cellar steps whacking it and whacking it with that broken piece
of broom until the broom broke again over the rat's back and still
it just kept going, now making its S's and question marks all over
the dusty cellar floor so that it looked like a thousand snakes had
been wrestling down there.

Jimmy kept thinking this had to be the momma rat. In fact
over the next year or so he'd *prayed* that what he had seen down
there had been the momma, and not one of her children.

The rat suddenly went straight up the cellar wall and into a
foot-high crawlspace that spread out under the living room floor.

"You get it, son?" His mother had called down from the
kitchen door, her voice shaking like his grandma's used to.

He started to call back that he'd lost it, when he looked up at the crawlspace, then dragged an old chair over to the wall, and climbed up on the splintered seat for a better look.

Back in the darkness of the crawlspace there seemed to be a solider black, and a strong wet smell, and a hard scratch against the packed earth that shook all the way back out to the opening where his two hands gripped the wall.

The scratching deepened and ran and suddenly his face was full of the sound of it as he fell back away from the wall with the damp and heavy black screeching and clawing at his face.

His momma called some people in and they got rid of the nests in the dressers and closets but they never did find the big dark momma he had chased into the cellar. At night he'd think about where that rat must have got to and he tried to forget what wasn't good to forget.

There was one more thing (*isn't there always*, he thought). They'd had a dog. Not back when he'd first seen the big momma rat, but later, because his momma had felt bad about what happened and he'd always wanted a dog, so she gave it to him. Jimmy named it Spot, which was pretty dumb but "Spot" had been a name that had represented all dogs for him since he was five or six, so he named his first dog Spot even though she was a solid-color, golden spaniel.

Just having Spot around made him feel better, although as far as he knew a dog couldn't help you much with a rat. Maybe she should have gotten him a cat instead, but he couldn't imagine a cat of any size dealing with that big momma rat.

Jimmy didn't think much about that dog anymore. Ah, Jimmy, thank you.

They had Spot four years. Jimmy was sixteen when the rats came back, a few at a time, and quite a bit smaller than the way he remembered them, but still there seemed to be a lot more of them each week and he'd dreamed enough about what was going to happen to him and his momma when there were enough of those rats.

Then he was down in the cellar one day when he saw this big shadow crawling around the side of the furnace, and heard the scratching that was as nervous and deep as an abscess. He ran upstairs and got his dead daddy's shotgun that his momma had kept cleaned and oiled since the day his daddy died, and took it down to the dark, damp cellar, and waited awhile until the scratching came again, and then that crawling shadow came again, and then he just took aim, and fired.

When he went over to look at the body, already wondering how he was going to dispose of that awful thing without upsetting his momma when she got home, he found his beautiful dog instead.

He'd started crying then, and shaking her, and ran back up the steps to get some towels (but why had she been crawling, and why hadn't she just trotted on over to him like she'd always done?), and when he got back down to the cellar with his arms full of every sheet and towel he could get his hands on, there had been all these rats gathered around the body of his dog, licking off the blood.

And now there were rats in his house, around his children.

The rat catcher, Homer Smith, was broad and rounded as an old Ford. Tess called Jimmy at work to tell him that the "rat man" had finally gotten there and Jimmy took the time off to go and meet him. When Jimmy first saw him the rat catcher was butt-wedged under the front porch, his big black boots soles out like balding tires, his baggy gray pants sliding off his slug-white ass as he pushed his way further into the opening until all of a sudden Jimmy was thinking of this huge, half-naked fellow crawling around under their house chasing rats. And he was trying not to giggle about that picture in his head when suddenly the rat catcher backed out and lifted himself and pulled his pants up all in one motion too quick to believe. Homer Smith was big and meaty and red-faced like he'd been shouting all morning and looking into his face Jimmy knew there was nothing comical about this man at all.

"You got rats," Homer Smith said, like it wasn't true until he'd said it. Jimmy nodded, watching the rat catcher's lips pull back into a grin that split open the lower half of his bumpy brown face. But the high fatty cheeks were as smooth and unmoved as before, the eyes circled in white as if the man had spent so much time squinting that very little sun ever got to those areas. The eyes inside the circles were fixed black marbles with burning highlights. "Some call me out to look at their rats and it comes up nothing but little mousies they coulda chased away their own selves with a lighter and a can of hairspray. If they had a little hair on their chests that is." Miranda's "mousies" sounded lewd and obscene coming from Smith's greasy red lips. "But rats now, they don't burn out so good. That hair of theirs stinks to high heaven while it's burning, but your good size mean-ass rat, he don't mind burning so much. And you, son . . ." He raised his fist. "You got rats."

Jimmy stared at the things wriggling in the rat catcher's fist: blind, pale and constantly moving, six, maybe eight little hairless globs of flesh, all alike, all as blank and featureless as the rat catcher's fingers and thumb, which now wriggled with the rat babies like their own long-lost brothers and sisters. "How many?" Jimmy asked, glancing down at his feet.

"How many what?" Smith asked, gazing at his fistful of slick wriggle. He reached over with a finger from the other hand and flicked one of the soft bellies. It had a wet, fruity sound. Jimmy could see a crease in the rat skin from the hard edge of the nail. A high-pitched squeak escaped the tiny mouth.

Jimmy turned away, not wanting to puke on his new shoes. "How many rats? How many days to do the job? Any of that," he said weakly.

The rat catcher grinned again and tossed the babies to the ground where they made a sound like dishrags slapping linoleum. "Oh, you got lots, mister. Lots of rats and lots and lots of days for doing this job. You'll be seeing lots of me the next few weeks."

And of course the rat catcher hadn't lied. He arrived each morning about the time Jimmy was leaving for work, heavy gauge cages and huge wood and steel traps slung across his back and dangling from his fingers. "Poison don't do much good with these kind o' rats," Smith told him. "They eat it like candy and shit it right out again. 'Bout all it does is turn their assholes blue." Jimmy wasn't about to ask the rat catcher how he'd come by the information.

If he planned it right Jimmy would get home each afternoon just as Smith was loading the last sack or barrel marked "waste" up on his pickup. The idea that there were barrels of rats in his house was something Jimmy tried not to think about.

If he planned it wrong, however, which happened a lot more often than he liked, he'd get there just as the rat catcher was filling the sacks and barrels with all the pale dead babies and greasy-haired adults he'd been piling up at one corner of the house all day. Babies were separated from the shredded rags and papers they'd been nested in, then tossed into the sacks by the handfuls, so many of them that after a while Jimmy couldn't see them as dead animals anymore, or even as meat, more like vegetables, like bags full of radishes or spring potatoes. The adults Smith dropped into the barrels one at a time, swinging them a little by their slick pink tails and slinging them in. When the barrels were mostly empty, the sound the rats made when they hit was like mushy softballs. But as the barrels filled the rats made hardly a sound at all on that final dive: no more than a soft pat on a baby's behind, or a sloppy kiss on the cheek.

Jimmy had figured Smith was bound to be done after a few days. But the man became like a piece of household equipment, always there, always moving, losing his name as they started calling him by Tess's name for him, "the rat man," as if he looked like what he was after, when they were able to mention him at all. Because sometimes he made them too jumpy even to talk about, and the both of them would stay up nights thinking about him, even though they'd each pretend to the other that they were asleep. A week later he was still hauling the rats out of there. It seemed impossible. Jimmy started having dreams about a mine tunnel opening up under their basement, and huge, crazy-eyed mine rats pouring out.

"I don't like having that man around my kids," Tess said one day.

Jimmy looked up from his workbench, grabbing onto the edge of it to keep his hands from shaking. "What's he done?"

"He hasn't *done* anything, exactly. It's just the way he looks, the way he moves."

Jimmy thought about the rats down in their basement, the rats in their walls. "He's doing a job, honey. When he's done with the job he'll get out of here and we won't be seeing him anymore."

"He gives me the creeps. There's something, I don't know, a little strange about him."

Jimmy thought the rat man was a lot strange, actually, but he'd been trying not to think too much about that. "Tell you what, I've got some things I can do at home tomorrow. I'll just stick around all day, see if he's up to anything."

Jimmy spent the next day doing paperwork at the dining room table. Every once in a great while he'd see the rat man going out to his truck with a load of vermin, then coming back all slick smiles and head nodding at the window. Then Jimmy would hear him in the basement, so loud sometimes it was like the rat man was squeezing himself up inside the wall cavities and beating on them with a hammer.

But once or twice he saw the rat man lingering by one of the kid's windows, and once he was scratching at the baby's screen making meow sounds like some great big cat, a scary, satisfied-looking expression on his face. Then the rat man looked like the derelicts his momma had always warned him about, the ones that had a "thing" for children. But still Jimmy wasn't sure they should do anything about the rat man. Not with the kind of rat problem they had.

When he talked to her about it that night Tess didn't agree. "He's weird, Jimmy. But it's more than that. It's the way the kids act when he's around."

"And how's that?"

"They're scared to death of him. Miranda sticks herself off in a corner somewhere with her dolls. Robert gets whiny and unhappy with everything, and you know that's not like him. He just moves from one room to the next all day and he doesn't seem to like any of his toys or anything he's doing. But the baby, she's the worst."

Jimmy started to laugh but caught himself in time, hoping Tess hadn't seen the beginnings of a smile on his lips. Not that this was funny. Far from it. But this idea of how the baby was reacting to the rat man? They called their youngest child "the baby" instead of by her name, because she didn't feel like a Susan yet. She didn't feel like anything yet, really—she seemed to have no more personality than the baby rats the rat man had thrown down outside the house. Tess would have called him disgusting, saying that about his own daughter, but he knew she felt pretty much the same way. Some babies were born personalities; Susan just wasn't one of those. This was one of those things that made mommies and daddies old before their time: waiting to see if the baby was going to grow into a person, waiting to see if the baby was going to turn out having much of a brain at all.

So the idea of "the baby" feeling anything at all about the rat man made no sense to Jimmy. He felt a little relieved, in fact, that maybe they'd made too much out of this thing. Maybe they'd let their imaginations get away from them. Then he realized that Tess was staring at him suspiciously. "The baby?" he finally said. "What's wrong with the baby?"

"Susan," Tess replied, as if she'd been reading his mind. "Susan is too quiet. Like she's being careful. You know the way a dog or a cat stops sometimes and gets real still because it senses something dangerous nearby? That's Susan. She's hardly even crying anymore. And you try to make her laugh—dance that teddy bear with the bright blue bib in front of her, or shake her rattle by her face—and she doesn't make a sound. Like she knows the rat man's nearby and she doesn't want to make a noise 'cause then he'll figure out where she is."

In his head Jimmy saw the rat man prowling through the dark house, his baby holding her breath, her eyes moving restlessly over the bedroom shadows. "Maybe he'll be done soon."

"Christ, Jimmy, I want him out of here! And I know you do, too!"

"What reason could I give him? We're just talking about 'feelings' here. We don't really know anything."

"What *reasons* do we need? We hired the man—we can fire him just as easy."

"Easy?"

"You're scared of him, Jimmy! I've never seen you so scared. But these are our *kids* we're talking about!"

"He makes me a little nervous, I admit," he said. "What you said about Susan makes me nervous as hell. And I am thinking about the kids right now, and how I can keep things safe for them around here."

"So we just let him stay? We just let him sneak around our kids doing God-knows-what?"

"We don't know he's doing anything except acting a little eccentric. We could fire him and the police could force him off our property, but that doesn't help us any with what might happen later."

"Later," she repeated. Jimmy couldn't bear how scared she looked. "What are we going to do?"

"I'm staying home again tomorrow. I'll park the car down the street and hide in the house. If he's doing anything he shouldn't he probably figures he can avoid your one pair of eyes. But tomorrow you'll be following your normal schedule and I'll be your extra pair of eyes. Between the two of us we shouldn't miss much." Jimmy looked down at the floor, thinking of the beams and pipes and electrical conduit hidden there. He listened for the rats, but the only scratches he heard were the ones inside his head.

The rat man came out exactly at nine in the a.m. like always. You could set your clock by him. He started unloading all his equipment, including the sacks and the metal barrel he threw the adult rats in. Jimmy crouched low by the master bedroom window, watching for anything and everything the rat man did. The first sign of weirdness, he thought, and he'd be hauling his kids' asses out of there. Tess went to work in the kitchen; they agreed it'd be best to pretend she was having a normal day.

The rat man disappeared around the corner of the house with the big metal barrel. Jimmy was thinking about shifting to another room when he came back, holding four stiff rats by the tails, their black coats grayed with dust. *No way he could've caught and killed them that quick,* he thought. The rats appeared to have been dead a good day at least. Jimmy watched as the rat man waddled up to the corner where the house turned into an "L," the corner with the window to the baby's room. He watched as the rat man dangled the stiff rats against the rusting screen, clucking and cooing, rubbing his fingers up and down the smooth, hairless tails, talking to Jimmy's baby through the screen and smiling like he didn't realize where he was, like he was off in another place entirely.

Off where dogs bleed in the dark and the rats gather round to lick the blood.

All day long Jimmy watched as the rat man sneaked dead adult rats and hairless baby rats out of his rusted green pickup and planted them in the crawl spaces under the house only to haul them out again and replace them in the barrel and the sacks. The same ones, over and over. Jimmy wondered how many rats they'd actually had in the first place. A dozen? Six? Four? Just the one, trapped back under Miranda's bedroom, and coming into the rat man's hand easier than a hungry kitten?

Now and then the rat man would come out with something wrapped in a towel or a rag, cradling it carefully in his arms like it was his own baby. Jimmy couldn't quite credit the gentleness he was seeing in the rat man; he looked silly, really. Jimmy wondered why the rat man would want some of the rats bundled up.

Right after the rat man left for the day Jimmy told the whole story to Tess. "I wasn't about to confront him on it here," he said.

"Well, if he's just a con artist then we can call the police."

"He's a helluva lot more than that—I think we've both figured that one. That little office he has in town is closed and there's no home phone number listed. So I'm going to have to go out to his place tonight. I'm going to tell him not to come around here anymore."

"What if he says no?"

"He's not allowed to say no, honey. I'm not going to let him."

"What if I say no, Jimmy?" Her voice shook.

"I don't think you're going to say no. I think you're going to be thinking about the kids, and that crazy man dangling rats in front of their faces like they were baby toys." He stroked her shoulder. After a few seconds she looked away. And Jimmy grabbed his coat and went out to the car.

The rat man lived out past the empty industrial parks on the north end of the city. Here the municipal services weren't so good, the streets full of ragged holes like they'd just run short of asphalt, the signs faded, with a permanent, pasted-on look to the trash layering the ditch lines.

It wasn't hard finding the right house. "The rat catcher man? He lives down the end of that street, *don't-cha-know.*" The old man was eager to tell him even more information about the rat man, but these were stories Jimmy didn't want to hear.

The rat man's house didn't look much different from any other house in that neighborhood. It was a smallish box, covered with that aluminum siding you're supposed to be able to wash off with a hose. A small porch contained a broken porch swing. There were green curtains in the window. A brown Christmas wreath hung on the front door even though it was April. Two trash cans at the curb overflowed with paper and rotten food. And the foot-high brown grass moved back and forth like a nervous shag carpet.

What was different about the rat man's yard was all the tires that had been piled there, stacked into wobbly-looking towers eight or nine feet tall, bunches of them sitting upright like a giant black snake run through a slicer, tangled together in some parts of the yard like a slinky run through the washer. Some of the tires were full of dirt and had weeds growing out of them. Some of the tires looked warped and burnt like they'd had to be scraped off somebody's car after some fiery journey.

But it was the nervous grass that kept pulling at Jimmy's gaze. It wiggled and shook like the ground underneath it was getting ready to turn somersaults.

When Jimmy moved through it on the way to the rat man's door it scratched at the sides of his boots. When Jimmy climbed the porch steps it slicked long, trembling fingers up around his ankles, making slow S-curves and question marks that set him shivering almost—it was crazy—with delight.

When Jimmy actually got to the door he could hear the layers of scratch and whisper building behind him, but he didn't turn around. The scratching got louder and Jimmy found himself angry. He started to knock on the rat man's door but once he got his hand curled into a fist he just held it there, looked at it and made the fist so tight the fingers went white. The scratching was in his ears and in his scalp now, and suddenly he was in a rage at the rat man, and couldn't get that picture out of his head: the rat man dangling those dead monster babies in front of Jimmy's baby's window.

He held back his fist before he punched through the rotting door and instead moved to the dingy yellow window at the back of the rat man's porch. He let go of the fist and used the open hand to shield his eyes from the late afternoon glare when he pressed his face against the glass.

He saw the rat man's back bobbing up and down like a greasy old sack moving restlessly with its full complement of dying rat babies. The walls of the room were lined with a hodge-podge of shelving: gray planks and old wooden doors cut into strips and other salvage rigged in rows and the shelves full of glass jars like his grandmother's root cellar packed with a season's worth of canning.

Jimmy couldn't tell what was in those jars. It looked like yellow onions, potatoes maybe.

The rat man was taking something out of a sack. He moved, and Jimmy could see a small table, and little bundles of rags on it. The rat man picked up the bundles gently and filled his arms with them. Then he headed toward a dark brown, greasy-looking door at the back of the room.

Jimmy stepped off the porch and moved toward the side of the house. The rat man's grass seemed to move with him, pushing against his shoes and rippling as he passed. He looked down and now and then saw a gray or black hump rise briefly over the grass tops before sinking down inside again.

The first window on that side was dark and even with his face pushed up into the dirty screen he could see nothing. A tall dresser or something had been pushed up against the window on the other side.

The second window glowed with a dim yellow light. Jimmy moved toward it, through grass alive with clumps and masses that rubbed against his boots, crawled over his ankles, and scratched at his pant legs.

A heavy curtain had been pulled across the window, but it gapped enough in the middle to give Jimmy a peep-hole. Inside, the rat man was unwrapping the bundles. Around the room were more shelves, but here they had been filled with children's toys: dolls, teddy bears, stuffed monkeys and rabbits, tops and cars and jack-in-the-boxes and every kind of wind-up or pull-toy Jimmy had ever seen. Some of them looked shiny brand-new as if they'd just come out of the box. Others looked as old as Jimmy and older, the painted wood or metal dark brown or gray with layers of oily-looking dust.

The rat man put his new toys up on the shelf: a Miss Raggedy Ella doll, Tiny Tears, Homer Hippo, G.I. Joe, a plastic Sherman tank, a baby rattle, and a teddy bear with a bright blue bib. Toys that belonged to Jimmy's kids. And then the rat man picked up the last, slightly larger bundle, and placed it in a pink bassinet in the middle of the room, where he unwrapped it and rearranged the faded blankets.

Suddenly Jimmy felt the rats clawing at his ankles, crawling up his legs.

He turned so quickly—thinking he'd run to the porch and break through the door—that he stumbled and fell on his knees. Instantly he had rats crawling up on his back, raking at his legs, several hanging by their claws and teeth from the loose front of his shirt. He stood and brushed them off him, finally grabbing one that just wouldn't let go with his hands around its belly and squeezing until it screamed and dropped.

All around him the towered and twisting mass of tires was alive with dark rats, scrambling over each other as they climbed and tumbled through the insides and over the outsides of the black casings. He didn't make it to the porch without losing a few hunks of skin here and there. *The rats gathered round to lick the blood . . .*

The rat man's door disintegrated the second time Jimmy plowed into it with his shoulder, but not without a couple of hard splinters lodging painfully into the top of his arm. He stumbled into the front room and crashed into the far wall where the shelves of old wood began pulling away from the wall, dumping row after row of Mason jars onto the floor.

His feet slid on the spilled gunk. He could feel soft lumps smashing under the soles of his shoes. He staggered and grabbed the edge of a shelf, bringing down more of the jars. He started moving toward the greasy brown door at the back of the room as if in slow-motion, looking down at his shoes and moving carefully so that he wouldn't slash himself on the broken glass, but all the time screaming, yelling at himself to get his ass in gear and get to that bedroom at the back of the rat man's house.

He saw, but didn't think about, the bodies of the hundreds of hairless little rat babies bursting open under his shoes and smearing across every inch of the wooden floor.

He felt himself sliding, beginning to fall, as he jerked the door open and headed down a pitch black hallway toward a dim yellow rectangle of light at the other end. He pushed at the invisible walls of the hallway to keep himself upright and raced toward that rectangle, the walls going away around him as in a dream.

He wasn't aware of pushing open the door to the back room. It just seemed to dissolve at the touch of his hands.

Homer Smith, the rat man, was bent over the pink bassinet, cooing and making little wet laughing sounds. Later Jimmy would wonder why it was the rat man hadn't paid any attention to the ruckus in the front part of his house.

Homer looked up, his hands still inside the bassinet, as Jimmy hit him across the face as hard as he could. He fell to his knees with a noise like thunder, then looked up at Jimmy, then looked around at all his toys, smiled a little, like he wanted Jimmy to play with him. *Off where the dog bled in the dark* . . . Jimmy kicked him in the ribs this time, with boots still smeared and sticky.

Homer doubled over without a sound, then he looked up at Jimmy again, and his face was as soft and unfocused as a baby's.

Jimmy thought about his baby in the bassinet, but couldn't quite bring himself to look yet. He glanced around the room instead and saw the broom propped in one corner. He stepped over to it, still aware that Homer wasn't moving, picked it up and brought it down across Homer's left cheekbone. The straw-end snapped off like a dry, dusty flower head and Jimmy used the broken handle to whip Homer's face until it was a bloody, frothy pudding, Homer's head snapping back and forth with each blow but still Homer stayed upright, leaning forward on his knees. Jimmy couldn't believe it, and it scared him something terrible.

He kept thinking about the baby, but couldn't keep his eyes off the baby catcher, the baby snatcher. Finally he took the ragged, broken end of the broom handle and held it a couple of feet from Homer's throat. Jimmy could feel the weight of the pink bassinet behind him, and the thing wrapped up inside it, not moving, not crying, keeping still as if watching to see what would happen, but Jimmy knew it wasn't just keeping still. It was dead. Susan was dead. He hadn't checked on her before he came out here after the rat man and he should have known, watching the rat man carrying all those swaddled objects out of his house like that. He should have *known*.

At last Homer Smith raised his bloody head and stared at the sharp stick Jimmy had poised at his throat and seeing what Jimmy was ready to do Homer began to cry a wet, blood-filled cry, like a baby, just like a baby Jimmy thought, and it reminded him of lots of things, not all of it bad, as he drove the sharp end of that stick as hard as he could into the soft skin of Homer's throat.

The dying took a few minutes, Homer trying to pull the stick out but not being able to. Jimmy threw up over by the bassinet until he had nothing left to heave. Finally he got to his feet again and stood over his baby, hesitated, then slowly unwrapped the blanket from around her.

And found two dead black rats there, curled around each other like Siamese twins. Homer had dressed each in baby doll clothes.

Jimmy felt the scratching up in his scalp, long and hard like fingernails clawing through a wooden door, long before he actually heard it. And then the sound of hundreds of pale tongues, lapping.

He turned and looked *off where the dog bled in the dark* at Homer Smith's body, and the hundreds of rats gathered round to lick the blood.

Rat Catcher: A Commentary

TEM IS AT HIS BEST WHEN HE LETS HIS PENCHANT for expressionism out of its proverbial cage, and "Rat Catcher"— which the author would categorize as an "ugly behavior" story about man at his most vile (rather than violent, *per se*)—is a perfect example of this. The story works on several levels, but what sticks with me most after reading it is the scene where our feckless narrator approaches the catcher's house on the other side of the tracks... and among all the squalor he encounters, he sees rats carpeting the entire yard in a writhing hoard of vermin. The narration delivers this observation in a brilliant but deadpan description that comes across as not merely believable, but somehow *normal* and *expected*, in the unfamiliar territory that Jimmy is entering.

Tem revels in psychological word-painting as a kind of philosophical musing. A lot of this story transpires inside the head of the narrator, but it is at this point where the internal world becomes externalized, giving us a word portrait of the protagonist's anxieties and fears—a method reminiscent of the background in Munch's masterpiece, "The Scream," which bends around the screamer as if it were attacking and suffocating him. One of Tem's outstanding talents as a writer is his talent for this kind of paranoid (if not borderline psychotic) depiction of Expressionism, one where our complicity with the viewpoint character only raises the fear factor for us, as everything is rendered uncanny and unstable, making us wonder what is and is not reality—what is and is not dream. Tem reminds us that, in fiction, these boundaries are arbitrary—and sometimes the root of the problem.

—Michael Arnzen, PhD

WHATEVER YOU WANT

THE CHRISTMAS SEASON WAS IMPOSSIBLE TO escape, gobbling up more of the calendar with each trip of the world around the sun. This year Trish was appalled to find Christmas aisles in the big box stores just days after the last "Trick or Treat!" of Halloween.

Little Bean was all of three now, but thanks to television able to recognize the holiday for the first time. She'd chattered on and on about "Santy Claws," one of the few clear phrases Trish was able to pick out of a stream of moist gibberish as Little B roamed their small apartment in unrepressed delight... and rage, if Trish ever said *no*. Anger or joy, Little Bean always seemed to be screaming.

Every mother Trish knew said, "Mine did the same thing. They grow out of it." Trish made an effort to believe them. "Don't take it personally." She tried to believe that too, even under a barrage of *I hate you!*s.

"Well, you asked for this." That's what her mother told her. Actually, she hadn't asked for this, not the deadening sameness of motherhood, the isolation of the single mom at the playground, the loss of a future she could now only imagine. Little Bean's dad was supposed to be doing this with her, but he'd wised up, skipped town. She wondered what kind of Christmas *he* was having.

It wasn't that Trish *hadn't* wanted a child. The truth was she just didn't know. And then she had one. And that child would cry and cry as if desperately wanting something she wasn't getting, but

Trish had no idea what it was. Was it because Trish secretly hated breastfeeding? Found it painful and somewhat disgusting, her child chewing on her like that? Was it because she'd never wanted to do this, at least not by herself?

Trish had a fleeting notion that one day Little Bean would suddenly start speaking, confessing that she could have told her mother what she had wanted at any time. She just hadn't cared to.

Little Bean wasn't the only person Trish had to please. She had her mother and father, grandparents, friends (at least the few that were left—a bunch had bolted once they realized Trish with a kid was far less fun than Trish without). She had sworn she wasn't going to wait until the last minute to shop, but here she was— Christmas Eve—frantically looking for a parking spot with her child screaming in the back seat.

She drove past the big malls. Their parking lots were full, cars prowling the lanes opportunistically, following shoppers walking out of stores with their arms full. She remembered an old mall farther out, scheduled to be torn down, but remaining open until the end of the holiday. Maybe she'd find unusual things there for the people on her list. They'd be impressed, especially with her having a difficult kid to take care of. It was already late afternoon. Another heavy snow waited in the night. The streets were flooded in steel gray fog.

The road out was poorly lit, with few houses along the way. The last rays of the setting sun made the distant woods appear on fire. An arc of tree limbs protruding from a snowbank resembled a partially buried giant spider.

Once past the worn-out welcome to the mall sign, construction barriers guided her through the main level of the old shopping complex. Orange cones and plastic webbing blocked everything. She descended a curved road to the basement level, parking crookedly between piles of debris, but so had everyone else. She got out and lifted B from her car seat. Her daughter thankfully was sound asleep. Trish remembered a vast amusement hall on this level. Now the windows were empty and greased.

A dark furry shape in the middle of the sidewalk turned out to be the burnt remains of a Christmas tree, a few soot-blackened balls dangling from its skeletal limbs. She was already feeling discouraged about finding anything good here, but she was running out of time. Too late to shop anywhere else, she was on a mission to find and buy.

Beneath broken concrete the ground moaned as if collapse were imminent. Some cracked exterior steps led to the main level. As darkness filled the risers the steps appeared to float in midair. B weighed almost nothing. When she got to the top she checked the blanket to make sure her daughter was still there. The child's face was pale, but her lips moved, as if whispering secrets Trish was not meant to hear.

Only a few weary-looking shoppers stared into the dimly-lit windows. An older man staggered past her, his overloaded bags hanging down and brushing the snowy sidewalk. His red Christmas sweater bore a giant white clown's face—big googly eyes over the nipples and a misshapen red nose, a wide crooked smile like a rip across the belly. He didn't appear to notice she was there.

There was a manger scene in a display window. Someone had replaced the baby Jesus with a dirty doll's head. The other figures were hunched with filth and looked less-than-human, their tiny faces dismayed. Skinny melting candles on either side leaned with dangerous possibility. A pile of rags on the sidewalk nearby stretched forth a hand clutching a can. The mouth splutter that followed might have been "please!" She gave the genderless arm a wide berth, sure it was a scam. She wanted to think the best of people but she was never up to the task.

A pile of dirty snow was studded with black stones, a water-logged scarf. It might have just been the remains of a good shoveling, but Trish thought she could make out a face. Dark figures hurried past the mall entrance. Some of them actually ran. "In a hurry for disappointment," she'd often heard her father say.

B stirred as they went through the doors. She thrust her blonde head out of the blanket looking startled. She began to cry, then stopped as she looked around.

"Down," she said, and Trish lowered her to the floor. She clutched three fingers of her mother's hand. Trish felt relieved. Maybe the kid would behave—she needed at least one thing to go right today.

"Toys?" B said weakly, as if afraid of the word.

"No toys today, Bean," Trish replied. "Santa will bring you some tomorrow. We can't be selfish every day—today we shop for other people."

"Santy Claws!"

"That's right, Bean," she replied, distracted. From this angle it was difficult to read the names of the stores. She had no choice but to go down each aisle and find some place still in business.

"Santy!" B cried again, and broke away, running straight ahead into shadows and dim light.

Trish stared for a moment, and then shouted, "Bean! Come back here!" She ran into the murkiness after her, furious. She had absolutely no control over the kid.

They were in some kind of central space, poorly lit, and half of it was blocked off where demolition had already begun. Trish was vaguely aware of a few shoppers circling the area, going in and out of shop doors that opened onto this space. Some were blackened silhouettes, like ambulatory fire victims.

Trish didn't even see the line of children until she ran into the tail end of it, and Bean, waiting with the others. She grabbed onto her little girl and started to pull her away.

"No, Santy!" Bean screamed, squirming.

"Can I help?" The voice was nearby and below her. Trish looked around. A very short old woman in an elf's cap much too big for her head stared up at her.

"I—there's not enough time." Trish was flushed, angry. "There are presents I just *have* to get."

"Leave her here and you can shop. We'll take care of her. She'll visit Santa Claus, and you'll get your shopping done unencumbered."

"Santa Claus?" Trish gazed up the line to its beginning. There was the big chair holding an old man swallowed up by a voluminous red suit. He appeared to be asleep as a small child chattered into his face. Santa's beard was long, but not very full. Large patches appeared to be missing, and that child, leaning so close to the old man, was eating them?

"But I can't just *leave* her here. *Can* I?" She looked back up at Santa. The next child in line crawled up into his unpromising lap. The old man startled, straightening up so quickly the child almost fell. The large reindeer nearby suddenly came to life—someone in costume—and jumped forward, but Santa had already steadied the child with his knobby hands.

"Don't you just *hate* Christmas? I know I do," the elf woman said. "People are *terrible*, and the little brats, aren't they just the *worst* this time of year?" The old woman's grin displayed many missing teeth.

"I... well, yes, sometimes." Trish looked down at B, whose eyes were fixed on Santa. "There's just never enough time. And it's not like I get to do anything fun, anything *I* want to do. It's really not fair."

"Do you know what your little girl wants for Christmas?" A new voice, another woman's. Trish turned and was appalled by the towering height of the figure. It was the costumed reindeer from Santa's side—how did she get here so fast? The reindeer suit had brown arms and legs and an enormous white bib covering the torso, a large grotesquely friendly reindeer head with wide-set eyes staring at some distant point in space.

"Everything, everything she sees on TV. She jumps up and down and goes crazy over every single toy commercial. She wants it all." Trish hated the way she sounded, but it was the truth.

"Don't we all," the little old woman said.

"That makes it easy," the voice inside the giant reindeer head replied. "I'll just have Santa tell her she'll get whatever she wants."

"Whatever she wants," Trish repeated. "Well, isn't that great. I'd just settle for getting what I deserve."

"Sometimes it's the same thing, don't you think? Go shop. We'll take care of her. Everything will turn out as it should. I promise. On my oath as a reindeer!"

Trish glanced at Bean, still transfixed, shuffling ahead with the other children. No other parents to be seen. She wouldn't even notice her absence. Her daughter was so self-contained—she cared nothing for Trish at all. "I'll hurry," she said, and turned away.

"Wait!" It was the old woman. Trish turned back around. "What do *you* want for Christmas? We'll put in a word for you with the old man. Anything."

But Trish had no time to think. "Just tell him whatever I want, whatever I deserve." She rushed off, relieved to have a few minutes of shopping time by herself. Bean's dad probably wasn't shopping—he probably wasn't even celebrating Christmas. He was probably just sitting in front of his TV drinking. Maybe that was sad, but Trish envied him.

The first place she went into was an antique shop, apparently, and the items—a messy clutter of metal and wood, paper and cloth—were poorly displayed. Of course they were *all* going out of business, so a handsome display no longer mattered. And it also didn't matter what she got the relatives, did it? Whatever she got them, Trish knew they would just politely nod—what was the point in trying to please them? She should just do all her shopping here.

A grubby artificial Christmas tree stood just inside the door of the shop. It appeared to have been repaired many times, branches taped or wrapped in graying string. A tiny bird's skull hung from one branch. Other items on the tree were so mossy with dust they were impossible to identify. Others were identifiable, but as inappropriate as the bird's skull—a kitchen whisk, dental floss, a comb—mixed with such traditional decorations as a ceramic angel, an antique star, some lovely blue and green globes.

Trish turned and glanced back at the distant Santa line, still moving slowly. She thought she recognized Bean's yellow jumper. With no sales clerk in sight she ventured deeper into the store.

Several collapsing cartons of grubby ornaments filled one table. The hand-lettered sign read "Seconds." She picked through a few, afraid to dig too deeply in case something nasty lay underneath. Each ornament was distorted in some way—imperfect spheres, lopsided egg shapes—irregular and shifting coloration. The softer ones resembled diseased organs.

An assortment of Jesus dolls—folk art—were gathered in a bin. They all looked like bad Jesuses to her. A box labeled "Fire Sale" was full of unidentifiable blackened things, all with hooks to hang from a tree.

In the central part of the store stuffed rats hung from a line stretched overhead. Most wore Santa hats.

"I had a bunch left over from Halloween, but it's the red caps what make them festive, dunnit you think?"

A thin man with a very wide grin peered down at her. His hair was black and slicked back and had rolls of dust—her mother called them woolies—decorating it here and there.

"Very . . . clever," she replied.

"Can I help you find what you want?" he asked.

"I'm not sure I know."

"Maybe, maybe not," he said. "Most of us actually do—we're just too afraid to say. We'll be closing soon, by the way."

Trish glanced away, uncomfortable. "I just need a few things, and then I have to go retrieve my daughter. She's visiting Santa."

"Are you sure? They haven't had a Santa in years." He moved a little closer. She could smell the oil in his hair. How could he not know? Santa was set up practically right outside his store.

Trish felt she should leave, but stopped herself. She'd be done in just a few minutes, and then she and the B could go home. "Well, they must have changed their minds. I have to hurry along." She went deeper into the shop, away from him and his greasy, dust-laden hair. She picked up a dusty old broach for her mother—she could clean it, and she'd get one of those defective ornaments for her father. They never liked anything she gave them anyway. And this, this would let them know exactly how she felt about this horrible holiday. Maybe they would stop expecting her to come—what a relief that would be.

But she still needed something for her sister, the cousins, and whoever else she'd probably forgotten. At the back of the store was a stack of Victorian Christmas cards. She began thumbing through them quickly, seeking something that might actually impress.

The first card to catch her eye bore a picture of an unhappy looking man in stocks being tormented by a jester. "Happy Christmas to You!" it proclaimed. In the next, a seriously wintry scene of ice and snow, a man was being mauled by an angry polar bear. On another there was some sort of bifurcated root thing with a human head wearing a top hat and monocle. A root branch stuck out like an arm, clutching a heart-shaped object with the message "A Merry Christmas to You." She held on to these—she didn't really understand them, but they still perfectly expressed everything she was feeling.

On one card a snow man had turned sinister and was threatening a little boy. And here were two dead birds, their feet pointing stiffly upward—"Merry Christmas and Happy New Year!" Then another, "May Christmas Be Merry," with a frog dancing with a hideous black beetle as a giant fly held aloft a golden ring. They were all suitably unpleasant. What a wonderful, wonderful shop!

On another card a hideous goat creature with long black fur, twisted horns, and a forked tongue threatened a tub full of babies with a giant fork. Was he really planning to skewer them? Maybe this one was too much. She would give it to her father.

"That be Krampus," the skinny clerk croaked at her elbow.

"Wha-at?" He'd scared her so bad she felt dizzy.

"Krampus. He's the opposite of the Santa Claus. He's the other one, the one what punishes the children who misbehaved during the year. Tortures them, I reckon. I've got loads of Krampus gear, if you're interested."

"No!" she cried. "What a terrible idea! Who'd want to invent such a thing?" Guiltily, she dropped the cards. She glanced at her fingertips—they were filthy. She quickly rubbed them on her sleeve.

"They invented him to protect the kiddies, I reckon. Keep them from getting into trouble. Sometimes you have to scare those little ones, just to make them behave. They can be like little animals, if you don't."

"No, no you don't!" she cried, and started for the door.

"Sometimes the truth is a scary thing."

She turned and stared at him. "What's that?"

"She needs something she's not getting, but the hateful creature won't tell you what it is. You didn't sign up for this, now did you? You didn't ask for this. This is not what you wanted at all." The clerk's face had gone dark, as had most of the shop.

"I have to go," Trish said, crying. "I have to pick her up."

"But it's too late for all that now," the clerk said, invisible, just a rough voice issuing from the dark. "You already made your choice. They're shutting us down. They're tearing down the mall."

"Who are *they-ey?*" Again the quake in her voice, the awful evidence that she was terrified.

"Why the ones what make the holidays. The ones what make the malls and then tears them all down. The ones what know all the rules in the rule books, but refuse to tell you what they are. The ones what takes the kiddies and does what needs to be done."

Trish ran from the store. "B—Bean!" She shouted at the dark. All light was gone except for a thin line of silver overhead illuminating a narrow shaft of bright dust. Or was it snow?

She wandered around in the thickening black calling her daughter's name, running into things, tripping over what might have been loose tiles or ceiling debris. Once she touched what she was sure were antlers, and begged Santa's assistant for help. But there was no answer. Feeling further down she realized it was just a head with nothing inside.

Eventually the dark ahead of her lightened into shadow, and then lightened again into an amber mist. She stumbled forward into a field where the mall used to be—after they tore it all down. The grass and the tall weeds were whitening gradually under a silencing fall of snow. There the distant trees whose edges still showed a glimmer of flame. There the collapsing haystacks and the broken fences. And then among the naked trees the worn and battered chair and the withered old man dressed in faded red hunched over a yellow bundle in his lap. He appeared to be mumbling something. Or was that just Trish, mumbling to herself?

"Please," she said, like that beggar she'd encountered earlier. "Please, there's been a misunderstanding."

He looked up at her, his beard torn apart, the surrounding skin raw and bleeding. He held the yellow bundle up. "No," he said. "You were asked whatever you wanted."

"But I don't *know* what I wanted! I never have!"

She rushed forward and yanked the bundle from his arms, holding it tightly against her chest as she ran.

She didn't look until later, when she had her child back safely in her car. She wept and apologized, and she promised all she would do to make up for her mistake. But the twisted and weathered log inside the bundle remained silent, although Trish could just make out the beginnings of a nose, and the lines of a delicate mouth, if she stared long enough into the cracked wood.

WHATEVER YOU WANT: A COMMENTARY

STEVE RASNIC TEM HAS GIVEN US ALL SOMETHING of a Christmas gift with his new and original contribution to this collection, and what an amazing story it is. "Whatever You Want" is a chilling and unforgettable psycho-dramatic allegory about an exhausted mother keening for a break from her hyperactive "little bean" of a child, and regretting the results when a mall is all-too willing to help her escape her parental burden while she shops for others in her family.

This is not merely the typical Christmas horror story of dark fable leaning; the narrative adeptly and overtly plays off the fears that all parents have about possibly losing a child in a busy shopping mall, while also mixing in a very real—but perhaps secret—desire that parents (especially mothers) have for independence and freedom from their never-ending responsibility, and the children who incessantly "chew on" them. Tem earns our identification and wonder just as he builds up to an O. Henry twist delivered via a rising sense of panic and dread that is masterfully rendered when the protagonist realizes what it is she (and "Santa") have unconscionably done. With a nod to ancient Pagan traditions of seasonal change and associated human sacrifice, here the child's life itself has been transformed—an allegory of the sacrifice—to become a Yule log, in the realization of a Christmas wish.

But for all its psychological depth and maternalistic terror, Tem's masterful manipulation of setting is what truly generates horror in this story. The decrepit shopping mall location is brilliantly described in a manner akin to a haunted house. At first it just seems a bit impoverished and neglected when the narrator arrives—perhaps a little haunted, even, in its broken concrete that "moaned as if collapse was imminent." But the longer the protagonist shops the stores, the stranger the shops and its population become, and Tem has a field day cataloguing this litany of weirdness that his protagonist encounters; there's a lot of humor and irony here. But soon it is not simply the concrete that is collapsing, but the walls of reality itself as the mother searches for her lost child among a thickening blackness of terror, and the orchestrations of the shopping mall Santa become satanically evident.

And more covertly, Tem's critique of the emptiness of consumer culture—and all its false promises to deliver "whatever we need"—is delivered with a biting touch of satire of *both* the mass marketplace (which the mall symbolizes) *and* the faux dreams of holiday rituals they package and sell to unsuspecting consumers. Our dreams and desires in that kind of system, ultimately, are no better than a stump of misshapen wood.

—Michael Arnzen, PhD

WHY STEVE RASNIC TEM

MATTERS

BY MICHAEL ARNZEN, PHD

IF YOU'VE ALREADY READ THE CONTENTS OF THIS primer, you know very well why Steve Rasnic Tem matters: Because he writes genre fiction that transcends expectations and aspires to be something else. I'm reluctant to call that something else "literary." Let's just call it *hyperreal*.

The reality of the world he creates for his characters in any given story somehow combines with the reality of our worlds as we read along. On some level, every Tem story I've read sutures me inside the mind of the narrator or protagonist, bringing me into a strange dream-like connection with a fictional ideation, and it's bewildering to me how he accomplishes this. His ability to integrate a reader into the story's dreamscape is not necessarily done in a metafictional way, in which the story is always about story itself. Stephen King does it that way in his novel, *Misery*, for instance, by not only giving us Paul Sheldon's feverish viewpoint of Annie Wilkes, but also including the *actual pages* from the *fictional* romance novel that Annie Wilkes forces him to write under duress—all of which is actually written by Stephen King— who also is a figment of our imagination. No, that kind of metafiction draws attention to the art of storytelling itself, asking the reader to contemplate how the reading experience is constructed, and whether our narrated realities can really be trusted when they are formed by language alone, all meaning teetering on the brink of collapse in fiction's virtual house of cards.

Meaning is indeed often teetering in this way in many Steve Rasnic Tem stories, which seem compelled to excavate beneath the surface veneer of reality to see what can be dug up, though Tem avoids the artifice of metafictional techniques and instead gleefully embraces the *psychodrama* of the fantastic. Tem's approach often experiments with structure, and he certainly does write about the nature of narrative within his stories (perhaps his recent novel, *UBO* (Feb, 2017) is a good example of that), but the experiment that dominates Tem's work is more psychologically-bound. It's more akin to Kafka than Lovecraft. He accomplishes his own brand of hyperreality by letting his narrators or protagonists speak from a point-of-view that goes deeper than most writers would dare—it's as if we're hearing thoughts from a confessional kind of psychological space, making us co-conspirators, in a fashion. Tem's talent is to be psychologically intimate with not merely the character's subject position, but more broadly he is concerned with dramatizing the character's emotional processing of the world that is constructed around the character... in a manner that is *especially* effective when that world is falling apart.

Take, for instance, the ending of his new tale, "Whatever You Want." Tem's protagonist, Trish, wants only to take a moment of respite from the holiday season and all the parental burdens that seem to come with it, leaving her child with the shopping mall Santa. We are placed in her subject's position as she reasons out what she is going to do at the mall, and we follow along with her as she idly shops and explores her newfound momentary freedom, with only minor twinges of parental guilt battling her deep desire for liberty. Her pang for freedom surely is a very common sentiment, one that invites our sympathy rather than damning judgment. But just when we get comfortable rooting for Trish, she realizes the implications of what she's done, and the world seems to fold in on her, confirming her paranoia. Our empathy is replaced by dread as she races back to retrieve her child, yet finds herself lost "in the thickening black calling her daughter's name, running into things, tripping over what might have been loose tiles or ceiling debris. Once she touched what she was sure were antlers..." The unfathomable abyss of a dark world much larger and different than she first assumed takes dominance over her mental landscape. The unexpected ("antlers") reveals itself with greater and greater frequency, but only peripherally as she struggles to orient her crumbling landscape. She ultimately stumbles into an "amber mist" that becomes "a field where the mall used to be—after they tore it all down" with "collapsing haystacks and broken fences... naked trees" and there encounters the weird operations behind her unexpected fate.

If you read closely, perhaps a second time, you might wonder: where is this field "where the mall used to be—after they tore it all down"? Is it cheating to skip ahead to a future, post-mall? No, because this is the extreme outcome of her act of leaving the child behind... just a few minutes is a sin equivalent to forever. And because the story's setting is constructed entirely in our mind as a figment of our imagination, Tem knows he is free to pull the carpet out from under his protagonist (and us), removing the mall altogether and revealing a stage of purely supernatural—that is to say *symbolic*—drama to transpire. The child she is handed, when all is said and done, is a stump of wood. Obviously, this is an O. Henry twist, in that "Whatever She Want[ed]" in the story may have been a passive, quiet, doll of a child. Perhaps that's the object the child always was to her in the first place. But it is also a comment on the outside world of our consumer culture, which the holiday season and shopping mall setting represents. The stumpy doll-child harkens very much back to a wooden toy from a by-gone era; the agricultural references—the "antlers" and the snow and the "field where the mall used to be"—are throwbacks to a pre-capitalist time period, when malls and advertising did not exist. So the story, while seeming to end in a future, post-mall reality, actually restores us to a past, nostalgic reality in the end. Time literally has been "gobbled up" by the holidays, as is indicated in the tale's opening paragraph.

These themes—the dangers of consumer culture, the fear of abandonment by (or, conversely the loss of) a loved one, and familial nightmares—are frequent touchstones in the work of Steve Rasnic Tem. In terms of family issues, usually we are given a psychodrama of parental anxieties about children or vice versa. In "Hungry" it all comes together in a remarkable way, when the prodigal, monstrous offspring returns home to the mother who bore it. Tem inverts the Freudian concept of the "vagina dentata," as well as the classic Oedipal fantasy of a return to the womb—instead, the mother enters the womb-like body of her son, climbing into her dangerous mouth, abandoning her judgmental husband and misery for a poetically-just reversal of maternal fortune. "Hungry" is a perfect psychodramatic allegory for mother-son love in the orthodox Freudian sense, but Tem's foregrounding of the child's insatiable hunger seems to both excessively reflect a mother's fear of being eaten alive—as mothers quite literally are when a child suckles breast milk—and also at the same time comment on the all-consuming passion and heartache of familial love. To avoid abandonment, to reconnect with the prodigal son, to escape her miserable relationship with her boorish husband, mother bonds with son in the most radical way imaginable. The over-the-top nature of the fantasy could be a critique of Freud's theories, by taking them to their absurdist extremes. Nourishment, symbolically provided through a recourse to cannibalism, and the extreme martyrdom of the mother, leaves us wondering if Tem is serious. But this is part of Tem's genius—he does not always preach his themes and he lets the psychodrama do the talking.

However, I choose to read the story in not only these Freudian terms, but also on the cultural level, as a critique of consumerism itself. The child's monstrous desire to eat is a literalized symbol of the American consumer, incessantly "hungry" for *more, more, more*. When Jimmy Lee leaves the house, he enters the system of capitalism, taking up a series of low-wage jobs, functioning as a walking garbage disposal for various places, culminating in his confession that one gig had him eating "metal junk—especially cars." Jimmy symbolizes consumption not because he purchases status symbols and such, but because he is like a machine able to digest factory-produced garbage. Jimmy's mouth is actually akin to the furnace at the end of the factory line—an ever-open mouth, ready to swallow whatever next industrial product comes down the line, regardless of value. But of course, this work also leaves him unsatisfied—alienated by his job, an *Other* to everyone, he returns home seeking the human contact and relations that the world of consumer capitalism can never adequately provide him. But the domestic space is never immune to capitalism; in the end, the consumer consumes his family.

Tem's best work brings uses the lens of dark fantasy or psychological horror to critique the impact of our contemporary culture on the family itself, representing a withering "American Dream" that only produces nightmares. From the shopping mall in "Whatever You Want" to the psychologically broken working class laborer who frustrates the bourgeois family in "Rat Catcher," Tem is hyper-attuned to the trade-offs we endure to pursue our desires, often at the cost of family, friends, and other human relationships. Perhaps nowhere is this critique of the economy more present in his work than "In These Final Days of Sales"—a difficult, but award-winning allegory for our advertising-saturated, consumer-driven society, which Tem literalizes as "a change in the human psyche itself. We have become the creatures in our dreams . . . poured into pleasing and biodegradable packaging."

The story dramatizes this very notion—that the normal

relationship between a consumer product and a consumer has been reversed. Emil, the story's lame and aging salesman protagonist, functions like a Charon, oaring us through the river Styx of this miserable world, allowing Tem to depict a fractured culture that is dying from the emptiness that results when economic exchanges no longer have any value, and everything is an empty gesture. Emil reproduces these gestures, but it does him no good—his home is empty and his bed has a layer "of dust as soft and thick as another layer of upholstery" on it. His personal car is "a dead machine, designed for the transportation of the dead … [its engine] ripped out ages ago." This is Marx's "alienated laborer"—a worker who is so disconnected from the products of his work that he feels like an empty machine compared to them— in the form of a salesman.

The "manufactured need" that underpins consumer culture is familiar to anyone living today, in a world saturated by commercials and advertising, a world where planned obsolescence allows manufacturers to constantly sell the next best thing, from computer software upgrades to the latest greatest automobile, as soon as the previous model dies off. And it is designed to. The inauthenticity of such a culture hinges, as Tem's tale reminds us, on an empty exchange value which is a kind of death. "In These Final Days of Sales" hints that we have planned our own obsolescence, particularly evident in the story's conclusion where the weary salesman tries to return to an authentic life in retirement by teaching the next generation, but finally falters when it comes time to pay for a candy bar, because he doesn't understand "this commerce thing."

At the beginning of this essay, I noted how Steve Rasnic Tem has a Kafkaesque talent for depicting rich psychodrama that immerses us in the character's worldview, and that this approach to storytelling is most dramatically poignant when that world is falling apart. Usually what is "falling apart" in his work is not only the setting, or the psychological walls of the characters, but also the culture in which his characters operate—from the cultural institutions attached to family and gender to the cultural systems in which value and power circulate, like consumer capitalism. These themes are projected through a genre lens that allows us to see our own fears and nightmares playing out through the absurd or extreme fantasy that Tem depicts. Part of what makes Tem so successful at this method—which works extremely well in the flash fiction and novella formats that he is known for—is the variety of his literary (and non-literary) influences. For instance, Steve Rasnic Tem is a long-standing student of science fiction; in the early stages of his long and award-winning career, he edited the science fiction zine *Umbral*, and produced *The Umbral Anthology of Science Fiction Poetry*. In the introduction to the latter, he interestingly discusses how the representation of fantasy, even in "outer space," required "adopt[ing] so-called poetic techniques in order to write the new science fiction of 'inner space'":

> Science fiction, like fantasy, has always been weaker in character development while at the same time a bit closer to archetypal imagery than other types of prose fiction. As this imagery was developed, explored and excavated, connections with the inner world of experience were found. And, in turn, the science fictional treatment of these images brought them back out into the outer world, allowing these dreams to transform the world (Tem, 1982, xii).

I think Tem brings this concern to the poems, prose poetry, and surrealist fiction he writes in the horror genre, as well. Our brains process reality through the "inner space" and, in process, these dreams transform the world. However, what might make Tem's horror distinctive from the SF poetry he describes in the passage above is that horror actually is strong in character development by virtue of its freedom to dramatize psychological torment and terror—through expressionistic psychodrama.

Thus, not only is poetry an influence on Tem, but so is the artistic movement of the expressionists—from painters like Edward Munch ("The Scream" being the iconic representation of Expressionism) to film makers like Orson Welles and F.W. Murnau and Robert Wiene. In expressionism, the internal state of mind of a character is "expressed" in such a way in which the external world around that character actually represents their interior emotion. Thus, a shadowy alleyway might represent a character's fear of pursuing a particular journey or task. Like these classic artists and filmmakers, Tem too uses words as a kind of expressionist paintbrush, not merely in his highly poetic writing style, but in his representation of character psychology. In his helpful essay for writers, "One View: Creating Character in Fantasy and Horror Fiction," Tem describes how he uses gestalt dream interpretation theory to structure an expressionistic landscape:

> The relationship between characters and their settings is the relationship those same elements have in dreams... every object in a dream is a piece of the dreamer. A chair, a table, a car, another human being—each would represent some aspect of the dreamer (Tem, 1989).

When we read a Steve Rasnic Tem story, we need to pay attention to these details... but it is not difficult, because he constructs a hyperreal experience where the interior of his characters are paying attention to the details as much as we are, trying to navigate a world fraught with terror, weirdness, death, and dread.

Most horror storytellers today are working in the mode of Poe—going after a "single desired effect": they want to trigger a stunning emotional response of total dread. But I think that is just the starting pistol's shot for Tem, who is working in the mode of what you might call "Poe-stmodernism." His stories are playful experiments that are as much about the construction of horror fiction itself as they are about the scary story before our very eyes. And Steve Rasnic Tem brings an aesthetic to the table that shares much with the literary writer's ambition to write stories that aren't *only* focused on conflicts that bubble up to a terrifying climax, but also about *identity crises* that climax in epiphany—where characters are transformed by their realization of something new about the universe and come to realize just how limited their perspectives were all along.

An "epiphany" is a kind of awakening. A "now I see the light" moment in a story. But often in Tem stories, these epiphanies are akin to something else—they are less about illumination than a terrifying recognition in the flickering flames of Hell. His stories reveal a character's transformation, when they come to a recognition of Hell: "And now I see the darkness."

If his exploration of "inner space" transforms the world, then Tem writes stories that hold some hope that fiction can transform our worldviews for the better, too. The psychodrama of Tem harbors a therapeutic kind of experience that helps the reader come to terms with their own darkness, as well as the sickness of the world at large. For this reason, perhaps above all, Steve Rasnic Tem matters.

REFERENCES

Tem, Steve Rasnic (ed.) (1982). *The Umbral Anthology of Science Fiction Poetry*. Denver, CO: Umbral Press.

Tem, Steve Rasnic. (1989) "One View: Creating Character in Fantasy and Horror Fiction." *How to Write Tales of Horror, Science Fiction and Fantasy* (ed. Williamson, J.N.). Cincinnati, OH: Writer's Digest Books.

In Conversation with Steve Rasnic Tem

ERIC J. GUIGNARD: Hi Steve, and great to chat with you here. Of the stories selected for this small collection, I'd been familiar with most for many years. However, I only recently read "In These Final Days of Sales" for the first time, but it spoke to me immediately as I come from a background of outside sales. The story—originally a standalone chapbook—is sorrowful yet whimsical, a satiric commentary, as well as a humorous, wistful fantasy. Your characters are frequently very quiet and mild mannered, risen to the status of marginalized anti-heroes while stuck in surreal (and atmospheric!) settings. Why are you drawn to write toward these characters? Are these the people in life you feel yourself drawn to, those trying to make their own ways against the rut of daily routines?

STEVE RASNIC TEM: An early major influence on me was Frank O'Connor's *The Lonely Voice*, one of the first lengthy studies of the short story form that came out in the early '60s. He focuses on Turgenev, Chekhov, Maupassant, Kipling, Joyce, Mansfield, a few others, and he talks about how members of "submerged population groups" are the ideal characters for short form fiction. These individuals are outcasts who, for whatever reason, are on the fringes of society. The irony for me, though, was that it seemed to me these were the ordinary people, the core of what most people were if you stripped away the polish, the social mechanisms most of us use to fit in and appear normal. If anything, they're pretty close to being an "everyman" for me. I often think of them as who I might have become if certain things had gone wrong in my life. They value many of the things I value, and share many of my obsessions, but perhaps they've been a bit less successful at making things work out for them.

Some people believe that characters such as these cannot sustain an entire novel—that readers want characters a bit more heroic if they're going to read about them for two hundred pages or more. I don't agree with that, although I admit these characters can sometimes be problematic at novel length. You have to do things to keep them interesting over the long haul. But as the center of a short story, I think these sorts of characters are perfection.

EJG: "The Last Moments Before Bed" remains one of my favorite stories that you've authored. Perhaps because you first wrote it for my anthology *After Death...* it feels more personal. But even besides that connection, the story itself is just beautiful and introspective, haunting and emotional. Really, meaningful emotions seem to fill all your writing, and I've long considered you to be a master of expressive prose, in which quiet tales are made powerful and memorable by the feeling you exude into them. Do you set out in advance with a certain emotion or tone to place your story in—outlining your own sentiments, so to speak—or do you let your feelings develop naturally as your write?

SRT: The writing process for most of my stories involves discovering what the emotional center is, and until I find that emotional center I feel there's not really a story yet. I often start with just a series of intriguing random thoughts or images, and I try to figure out who it is that would think these things, or who it is that would see things in this particular way. So words, descriptions, dialog, characters, events, etc. accumulate. And there's almost always a theme, or a subject that comes with the initial story notion from the very beginning. And as all this evolves I'm constantly looking for that emotional center—what the viewpoint character is feeling about whatever is going on, because in my experience it's the conviction of emotion that gives things meaning. Once I pin that down, that often dictates the first rewrite—I go back to the beginning and begin rewriting with this emotional aspect in mind. It tends to change the prose considerably.

EJG: I've always most admired authors, such as yourself, who can write across genre boundaries. Horror, noir, science fiction, fantasy, thriller, and the nebulous "weird," not to mention your literary works, experimental pieces, poetry, and nonfiction: There's little you haven't tried your hand at. What drives this? Do you write whatever compels you on a given day, or do you search for different styles to experiment with for the sake of experience, or are there many and varied other reasons?

SRT: I suppose it comes from a somewhat old-fashioned idea of the writer—that the writer writes all forms, all genres from fiction to nonfiction, from poetry to drama, essays, criticism, etc. Being able to create work in all these forms and formats strengthens your vocabulary of approaches, and builds your repertoire of strategies. When a new idea comes along you then have all the tools you need to find a suitable treatment for that idea. Without that general experience you're limited in what you can do. And each of these kinds of writing strengthens the others. Writing nonfiction can strengthen structure and clarity. Writing fiction can loosen the imagination. Writing in different genres allows you to see the strengths in each, and to find new combinations of genre which better reflect your particular creative vision of the world. Not to mention that it's fun to sell work in a new form, to surprise yourself by getting into a venue you'd never expected.

EJG: Along this line, what inspires you creatively?

SRT: Just about everything inspires me creatively. I've become accustomed to transforming everything I experience into creative work. I especially love visual art, and drawing and painting has always been an important part of my creative process. It's one of the ways I work out imagery. I also love movies, and I usually see at least two or three in the theaters every week, not to mention all the ones I watch on TV, stream from the internet, or on DVDs and Blu-rays.

I also get inspiration from just watching anyone doing something extremely well—musicians, singers, chefs, dancers, athletes, builders. All these activities have a strong creative aspect, and observing them feeds and inspires my own creative process.

EJG: "Whatever You Want" is terrifying on a poignant level. I think everyone has had those moments where they're so overwhelmed and frustrated by a loved one—especially an irascible child—they sometimes wish circumstances were changed and that person were gone, though deep down knowing if they actually had the choice presented, they'd never willingly rid themselves forever of him or her. You explore frequently the significance of difficult decisions and the resonant impact of loved ones seemingly taken away by the forces of someone else's hand (as also seen in "The Giveaway"). How much do real world events or fears weigh into this, or is this a motif inspired by news or historic events or other causes?

SRT: I'm a parent and grandparent. I've had five children and currently have six grandchildren. So family is extremely important to me. Being a parent is complicated. Just being in a family is complicated, whether it's close-knit or emotionally distant. I have a lot of human relationships to draw on, a lot of personal fears and anxieties, a lot of memories, a great deal of loss. I also watch other people with an empathetic point of view. I try to put myself in their shoes, however different they may seem to be from me. A great deal of fiction writing is about empathy, and I believe if you have a problem with empathy you'd better get some if you're going to write fiction. You have to learn, somehow, how to love your characters. You have to see their humanity. That doesn't mean you approve of everything they do. But if you spend all your time writing about people you don't like, it's going to damage your work.

EJG: What else fills your days besides writing, especially now that you've recently retired from a Technical Writing day job (and congratulations, again, on that!)?

SRT: I have a schedule. I think that's important when you get to be sixty-six and retired from the day job. I go to bed 11 to 11:30 every night. I get up around 8. I exercise for an hour, eat breakfast, shower, then get in a couple or three hours writing. I eat lunch, then I take a nap. I never miss my nap. After the nap I may write, or visit someone, or do some art, or go to a movie, or read—it all depends. At night it's TV and internet, maybe some more writing, maybe not. I'm not trying to be more productive at this stage in my life—I figure I've been productive enough. I'm actually trying to produce a little less, but enjoy it more. Weekends I'm a little more flexible—I may sleep late, or get wrapped up in a book, go see kids and grandkids. I always go out to the movies Friday night, and get another one in Saturday or Sunday. I live life—it's a precious gift.

EJG: You've been selling short fiction since about 1976. How has the publishing industry changed over this time? Do you find current conditions more welcoming and/or propitious for horror authors or more challenging and/or apathetic?

SRT: There are more venues for getting published, and more ways of getting published. But there aren't more good paying venues, and of course fiction rates haven't kept up with inflation, not by a long shot. And having more ways of getting published hasn't been completely a good thing. There seems to be less reason for new authors to stick it out through the stressful and sometimes humiliating submission-and-rejection process, or the process of working your way from lower paying markets to higher paying ones. It's awfully tempting to forego all that and just self-publish. There's nothing wrong with self-publishing if you use it correctly—as one aspect of your publishing output but not all of it. The problem with entirely skipping the traditional publishing process is that it's the primary process out there for building a name, a reputation, and a career. Skip that and you're likely to have a much tougher time getting established. There are exceptions of course, and not everybody really cares about getting established. But it's something to consider.

As far as horror specifically, written horror fiction has for the most part a niche audience. I believe the '80s horror boom and the general popularity of horror was an aberration. It may happen again, but I doubt it. It will always be published, but generally in smaller numbers. It's another reason to try to conceptualize your work as your own genre. Be someone who transcends niches instead of being stuck in a niche.

EJG: What are some of the trends you see (or foresee) in horror fiction or, in a general sense, genre fiction, today?

SRT: I think serious work generally reflects the times it was written in. It's a kind of testimony as to how it was for you during your time on the planet. So I'd like to see horror fiction that reflects some of the chief causes for our anxiety: our divisive political environment, people's inability to come to terms with race, climate change and the destruction of the environment, and ultimately, our world. There'll be escapist stuff too, certainly, but I'm just not that in to escapist literature.

EJG: If you had the attention of the world for one moment, what would you say?

SRT: I used to think about this question when I was younger, not so much anymore. Most of the big general statements have already been said, haven't they, a thousand times or more? So I don't think I'd have anything to say. I'd just want people to read the stories, because most everything I know and feel is in the stories, and those can't be summarized that succinctly.

EJG: What does the future hold for Steve Rasnic Tem's writing career?

SRT: I have no idea really. My most ambitious, most important novel just came out—*UBO*, a meditation on violence. *Yours to Tell: Dialogues on the Art & Practice of Writing*, from Apex Books, also just came out. Melanie and I put almost everything we know about writing fiction into that book. I've also been lucky enough to get most of the stories of mine I really wanted to collect, collected. Those three things together make a pretty good capstone on a career.

Of course I'm still not done. At some point I'd like to get a "Best of" or "Selected" story collection out. And a collection of some of the newer stuff. Maybe a cross-genre collection of all my regional Appalachian stories. I'm working on a science fiction novel now, and there's another horror novel or two to be written. Maybe a dark crime novel. And hopefully more stories. Most of all, I'd like to surprise myself.

EJG: Thanks Steve, and I know many who would certainly hope you get all those potential works completed and into the hands of your fans!

(April 14, 2017)

THE SUBJECT MATTER OF HORROR: AN ESSAY

BY STEVE RASNIC TEM

A TYPICAL QUESTION POSED OF WRITERS OF HORROR (pointedly at times by non-fans of the genre) is, "Why do you write about such things?" A more difficult and basic question, I think, is the one which asks, "So what do you write about?"

Writers and long-time fans of the genre always seem to know the answer to this question—perhaps they think that answer should be all too obvious. Of course they know what the subject matter of horror is. "Well, I know it when I see it," they say, or perhaps they list archetypal figures, settings, themes: vampires, werewolves, ghosts, serial killers, nameless dreads, haunted houses, phantom ships, madness, decay, loss of faith.

I must admit that I don't always know. But I still experience some dissatisfaction with the way the subject matter of horror seems to be defined by so many writers, publishers, and book packagers in the field. Looking at much of the current product, one might conclude that horror is a genre of limited theme and variation, with a one-note emotional range (fear) which it plays quite into the ground.

Or could it be that the transformation of horror into a "genre" has in itself created these limitations?

Douglas Winter puts it well in the anthology *Prime Evil* when he says, "Horror is not a genre, like the mystery or science fiction or the western. It is not a kind of fiction . . . Horror is an emotion."

But defining that emotion of horror is not easy. And it is here, I think, that much of horror fiction loses its ambition. Most commonly, that emotion of horror has been equated with "fear," what Lovecraft called "the oldest and strongest emotion of mankind." The words "horror" and "fear" are often used interchangeably. Horror has been referred to as "the literature of fear." I think this has been a mistake.

This is not to say that "fear" does not play an important role. And at the lowest level of the horror reading experience, the writer often tries to shake the reader with fear. In many ways fear is an easily accessible emotion to write about. But it is only one emotional element in the texture of the experience that is horror. At its best, horror deals with the range of feelings—awe, terror, compassion, fear—which people experience when faced with the darkness of existence.

Horror, I believe, is a much more recent emotion in the psyche of the human animal than such primal responses as fear and anger. Fear and anger possess a certain physiological functionality in their origins (flight and fight). Horror has a much stronger psychological component, and perhaps began in the form of a very rudimentary sort of self-reflection. (Dogs, for instance, may experience both fear and anger, but I do not believe that they are capable of experiencing horror.)

Fear enables us to run away from danger. Anger spurs us to fight and defend ourselves. It may be that the ability to experience horror prevents more of us from turning into killers. Perhaps it also aids us in achieving some sort of balance when faced with our own mortality and that of the ones we love.

Do serial killers experience horror? I suspect most do not.

As a somewhat vague beginning, let us say that horror is a complex emotional reaction to dark areas of human experience. We may assume that these dark areas include the human being's capacity for violence and cruelty, the anticipation of one's own death, the fear of pain and loss. But it is the horror writer's job to recognize that the darkness shifts, that the shadows do not lie across the same regions for everyone, and sometimes the writer must seek out and find—or even anticipate—the new darknesses as they develop in our culture.

It is also commonplace to assume that a person's reaction to these various darknesses will be a fearful jump, in some instances a full-fledged terror. Yet how often do we react so simply to the true darknesses of "real" life?

It is my belief that "a literature of fear" describes only the most simple-minded horror fiction. And I think that a single-minded intention to create fiction which will "scare" the readers has led to the production of so much unreadable work in the field.

We may respond to the darkness of the unknown with unease and apprehension. We may respond to the darkness revealed with religious or philosophical awe. We may respond to the darkness of actual or anticipated loss with numbing grief. We may respond to the darkness of human cruelty with shame, and the shock of self-recognition. We may respond to the darkness of our own approaching death with anger, pity, reverence, and yes, even fear.

The best horror draws on a number of these emotions. It is in their interplay that horror occurs.

As in any literature of complexity, emotions in good horror fiction are heightened in relationship to each other. Often the strength and complexity of the horror is directly proportional to the strength of the love and fellow human feeling evoked in the piece. The intense passion of terror is a direct development of the writer's, and reader's, compassion for the characters.

In those tales in which the darkness is suddenly and miraculously revealed, resulting in the awe experienced in some classic ghost stories, or in Clive Barker's best examples of reality-revising "anti-horror," a hunger for vision and revelation must first be established.

Intrinsic to the creation of horror, I think, is an attempt to integrate a direct confrontation with our darker apprehensions. In horror we aspire to see the dark both as part of the everyday and as a realm which goes beyond the everyday, not something to be suppressed or by which to be overwhelmed. If horror has a larger developmental purpose in the consciousness of an individual or a society, then perhaps this is it—to end the estrangement between the experiences of dark and light, so that living a life "in pieces" might not be necessary.

Horror, I believe, is an emotion most of us need. Most of us, including the healthiest of us, have blocked and suppressed the darker aspects of human existence. Sometimes we may even go so far as to consciously decide that these dark areas have no function in our lives. But when this darkness is faced, even metaphorically, I believe that a certain sense of liberation occurs which is healthy for people—it is the liberation of integration, the relief that comes when we realize that no more dirty, closeted secrets remain.

But this liberation should not be confused with the "morbid fascination" some people indulge themselves in, and which writers of horror are often accused of (for the most part mistakenly, I think). Morbid fascination with dark materials is characterized by a kind of self-punishment. These are the readers who appear to flagellate themselves with the horrible aspects of life. No self-integration takes place because none is desired. The context of fellow human feeling for the horror experience is lost on such readers because they have cut themselves off from their fellow human beings. They are interested only in the dark.

Bad horror tends to encourage this perversion. The simple-mindedness of bad horror fails to liberate because it does not provide the complex emotional context and materials to make integration possible. In fact, bad horror aids readers in their avoidance because it isn't about anything central to the human conflict. Like a drug, bad horror fiction further distances readers from their true apprehensions, at times to the point of making these feelings almost inaccessible.

There was a time before the formulaic marketing of horror when a reader had to seek out the experience of horror in the available reading material. In the world before the time of a "Horror" category label printed on a book's spine, or painted in dripping letters across a book's cover, horror might be discussed as simply one aspect of literature or of an individual work, whether it was in the work of a John Fowles, a Kafka, a Kosinski, a Jim Thompson, or a Fuentes. Perhaps the horror was the most interesting aspect of a specific work, but it was heightened, made more effective, within the context of other concerns. One might go so far as to say that this "buried" horror had more to do with the experience of being human than do the garishly-packaged works we see so often today. The average horror novel today seems to have little to do with the conflicts of the human heart, and is more often just another facile presentation of predigested horror icons.

The creation of a horror marketing category has provided more of us with an opportunity to sell our work, but in an aesthetic sense it has damaged the literature as a whole. Although the arrival of horror packaging has focused a great deal of creative attention on this writing, it has also worked to simplify it, to reduce it to its lowest common denominator, in effect to dumb it up.

However, I don't look for the clock to turn completely back. I am looking forward to the day when the word "Horror" disappears from book spines. But I would have little problem with a less formal categorization to help readers find their way to what used to be called horror fiction: Say an imprint which specializes in a wide range of "dark" fiction, or in a particular collection of authors who tend to write about dark concerns. I also wouldn't mind if the covers of these books evinced a certain darkness or reality distortion, as long as the covers did not make the contents of these books more predictable.

What I would like to see is a redefinition of the horror category which focuses more on the larger human context of the horror emotion and less on the more transitory images which are used to express this emotion. Current horror writing and publishing have tended to confuse image with content, apparently thinking that merely populating a novel with vampires say, or werewolves, will make it the quintessential horror novel. I don't believe it does.

Breaking the monolith the horror category has become might enable editors to select a much wider range of material. Writers might be encouraged to loosen their own ideas of just what is the subject matter of horror. Writers might focus more on the broader, human emotional experience that horror entails.

And writers might become better qualified to probe the darker conflicts of the human heart.

He Made His Living writing Fairy Tales...

A BIBLIOGRAPHY OF
ENGLISH LANGUAGE FICTION
FOR STEVE RASNIC TEM

FOLLOWING IS A COMPLETE BIBLIOGRAPHY OF ENGLISH language fiction for Steve Rasnic Tem through Spring, 2017. Not included are: foreign language, individual pieces of non-fiction, or individual pieces of poetry.

Abbreviations Used:

(1) = indicates story's first publication. Omitted if story first published in author collection.

(c) = indicates the collection containing this story. If the collection is listed first, the story's first appearance was in this collection.

(r) = indicates this is a reprint appearance.

anth. = anthology

mag. = magazine

f.c. = fiction collection

ed. = edited

v. = magazine volume number

= magazine issue number

SHORT FICTION

"**2** PM: The Real Estate Agent Arrives"
>   (1) *Crimewave 10: Now You See Me* (anth., ed. Andy Cox): TTA
>   Press, 2008.
>   (r) *Best New Horror 20* (anth., ed. Stephen Jones): Running Press,
>   2009.
>   (c) *Ugly Behavior* (f.c.): New Pulp Press, 2012.

"**12** Minutes of Darkness"
>   (1) (chapbook insert, dually published with chapbook, *Celestial
>   Inventory*): Chris Drumm (Drumm Booklet), 1991.
>   (c) *Onion Songs* (f.c.): Chomu Press, 2013.

"**A**bsences"
>   (1) *Absences: Charlie Goode's Ghosts—Haunted Library "Psychic
>   Sleuths' Booklet Number Two"* (chapbook including 6 stories):
>   Haunted Library, 1991.
>   (c) *The Far Side of the Lake* (f.c.): Ash-Tree Press, 2001.

"**A**dleparmeun"
>   (1) *Cold Shocks* (anth., ed. Tim Sullivan): Avon, 1991.
>   (c) *Out of the Dark: A Storybook of Horrors* (f.c.): Centipede Press,
>   2016.

"The **A**doptions"
>   (1) *Drabble II—Double Century* (anth., ed. Rob Meades and David
>   Wake): Beccon Publications, 1990.
>   (r) *The Devil's Wine* (anth., ed. Tom Piccirilli): Cemetery Dance
>   Publications, 2004.

"**A**fter the Night"
>   (1) *After Hours* (mag., #25): William G. Raley, Winter 1995.
>   (c) *Out of the Dark: A Storybook of Horrors* (f.c.): Centipede Press,
>   2016.

"**A**fter Work"
>   (1) *Horrors! 365 Scary Stories* (anth., ed. Stefan R. Dziemianowicz,

Robert H. Weinberg, and Martin H. Greenberg): Barnes &
Noble Books, 1998.

(c) *City Fishing* (f.c.): Silver Salamander Press, 2000.

"Again, the Hit and Run"

(1) *Chrysalis 9* (anth., ed. Roy Torgeson): Doubleday, 1981.

"Alan's Mother"

(1) *Rod Serling's The Twilight Zone Magazine* (mag., v.1, #11): TZ
Publications, June 1982.

(r) *100 Wicked Little Witch Stories* (anth., ed. Stefan R.
Dziemianowicz, Robert H. Weinberg, and Martin H.
Greenberg): Barnes & Noble Books, 1995.

"Almost a Legend"

(1) *Hills of Fire: Bare-knuckle Yarns of Appalachia* (anth., ed. Frank
Larnerd): Woodland Press, 2012.

"Among the Living"

(1) (novelette): Delirium Books, 2011.

(c) *Absent Company* (f.c., ebook): Crossroad Press/Macabre Ink,
2014.

"Among the Old"

(1) *Pulphouse: The Hardback Magazine* (mag., #1): Pulphouse
Publishing, Fall 1988.

(c) *The Far Side of the Lake* (f.c.): Ash-Tree Press, 2001.

"Ancient Grass"

(1) *After Hours* (mag., #7): William G. Raley, Summer 1990.

"Andrew"

(1) *Palace Corbie 7* (anth., ed. John Marshall and Wayne Edwards):
Merrimack Books, 1996.

(r) *The Best of Palace Corbie* (anth., ed. Wayne Edwards): Stone
Dragon Press, 1999.

(c) *Out of the Dark: A Storybook of Horrors* (f.c.): Centipede Press,
2016.

"**A**ngel Combs"
> (1) *The Anthology of Fantasy & The Supernatural* (anth., ed. Stephen Jones and David Sutton): Tiger Books International, 1994.
>
> (r) *The Year's Best Fantasy and Horror: Eighth Annual Collection* (anth., ed. Ellen Datlow and Terri Windling): St. Martin's Griffin, 1995.
>
> (r) *Gamut* (online media): gamut.online, Feb. 2017.
>
> (c) *City Fishing* (f.c.): Silver Salamander Press, 2000.

"**A**partment B"
> (1) *Nightscript II* (anth., ed. CM Muller): Chthonic Matter, 2016.

"**A**phasic World Syndrome"
> (1) *Pindeldyboz* (online media): pindeldyboz.com, Nov. 2007.
>
> (c) *Onion Songs* (f.c.): Chomu Press, 2013.

"**A**quarium"
> (1) *Seaharp Hotel (Greystone Bay Chronicle 3* (anth., ed. Charles L. Grant): Tor, 1990.
>
> (r) *The Mammoth Book of Best New Horror, Vol. 2* (anth., ed. Stephen Jones and Ramsey Campbell): Carroll & Graf, 1991.
>
> (c) *The Far Side of the Lake* (f.c.): Ash-Tree Press, 2001.

"**A**rchetype"
> (1) *NonStop Science Fiction Magazine* (mag., #2): NonStop Press, Winter 1995.
>
> (c) *Onion Songs* (f.c.): Chomu Press, 2013.

"The **A**rtist and His Mother"
> (1) *Paradox* (mag., #13): Paradox Publications, Spring 2009.

"The **A**ssassination"
> (1) *Center* (mag., #9): *unknown publisher*, 1976.

"**A**t Play in the Fields"
> (1) *Solaris Rising* (anth., ed. Ian Whales): Solaris, 2011.
>
> (c) *Twember: Science Fiction Stories; Imaginings vol. 7* (f.c.): NewCon Press, 2013.

"At the Bureau"

(1) *Shadows 3* (anth., ed. Charles L. Grant): Doubleday, 1980.

(r) *100 Great Fantasy Short Short Stories* (anth., ed. by Isaac Asimov, Terry Carr, and Martin H. Greenberg): Avon, 1984.

(r) *100 Hair-raising Little Horror Stories* (anth., ed. Al Sarrantonio and Martin H. Greenberg): Barnes & Noble Books, 1993.

(r) *The Best of Shadows* (anth., ed. Charles L. Grant): Doubleday, 1988.

(c) *The Far Side of the Lake* (f.c.): Ash-Tree Press, 2001.

"At the End of the Day"

(1) *Dead End: City Limits* (anth., ed. David B. Silva and Paul F. Olson): St. Martin's Press, 1991.

(r) *The Year's Best Fantasy and Horror: Fifth Annual Collection* (anth., ed. Ellen Datlow and Terri Windling): St. Martin's Griffin, 1992.

(c) *The Far Side of the Lake* (f.c.): Ash-Tree Press, 2001.

"Attached"

(1) *Kayak* (mag., #60): *unknown publisher*, 1982.

(c) *Onion Songs* (f.c.): Chomu Press, 2013.

"August Freeze"

(1) *Weird Tales* (mag., v.49, #2): The Bellerophon Network, Inc., Winter 1985.

"Back Among the Shy Trees"

(1) *Shadows & Tall Trees 2* (anth., ed. Michael Kelly): Undertow Publications, 2011.

(c) *Here With the Shadows* (f.c.): Swan River Press, 2014.

"Back Windows"

(1) *Gauntlet* (mag., #1): Barry Hoffman, 1990.

"Bad Dogs Come Out of the Rain"

(1) *Horror Garage* (mag., #2): Under the Volcano, 2000.

(c) *Out of the Dark: A Storybook of Horrors* (f.c.): Centipede Press, 2016.

"The **B**ad People"

(1) *Fantasy Tales* (digest, v.7, #13): Stephen Jones, Winter 1984.

(r) *The Best Horror from Fantasy Tales* (anth., ed. Stephen Jones and David Sutton): Robinson, 1988.

(c) *The Far Side of the Lake* (f.c.): Ash-Tree Press, 2001.

"The **B**attering"

(1) *Shadows* 8 (anth., ed. Charles L. Grant): Doubleday, 1985.

(c) *City Fishing* (f.c.): Silver Salamander Press, 2000.

"**B**e Mine"

(1) *14 Vicious Valentines* (anth., ed. Martin H. Greenberg): Avon, 1988.

"**B**eautiful Strangers" (with Melanie Tem)

(1) (chapbook): Roadkill Press, 1992.

(c) *In Concert* (with Melanie Tem) (collection of collaborations): Centipede Press, 2010.

"**B**edtime Conversation"

(1) *Savage Kick* (mag., #6): Murder Slim Press, 2012.

(c) *Out of the Dark: A Storybook of Horrors* (f.c.): Centipede Press, 2016.

"**B**edtime Story"

(1) *Black Static* (mag., #32): TTA Press, Jan./Feb. 2013.

(c) *Out of the Dark: A Storybook of Horrors* (f.c.): Centipede Press, 2016.

"**B**ees from the Hive" (with Melanie Tem)

(c) *In Concert* (with Melanie Tem) (collection of collaborations): Centipede Press, 2010.

"**B**enjamin"

(c) *Out of the Dark: A Storybook of Horrors* (f.c.): Centipede Press, 2016.

"The Bereavement Photographer"
-   (1) *13 Horrors: A Devil's Dozen Stories Celebrating 13 Years of the World Horror Convention* (anth., ed. Brian Hopkins): KaCSFFS Press, 2003.
-   (r) *The Mammoth Book of Best New Horror, Vol. 15* (anth., ed. Stephen Jones): Carroll & Graf/ Running Press, 2004.
-   (c) *Celestial Inventories* (f.c.): ChiZine Publications, 2013.

"Between the Pilings"
-   (1) *Innsmouth Nightmares* (anth., ed. Lois H. Gresh): PS Publishing, 2015.
-   (r) *The Best Horror of the Year Volume 8* (anth., ed. Ellen Datlow): Night Shade Books, 2016.
-   (r) *Gamut* (online media): gamut.online, 2017.

"Bingo Thompson's Flying Cat"
-   (1) *Stories from the Hearth* (anth., ed. Brian Hatcher): Woodland Press, 2011.

"Bite"
-   (1) *The Horror Show* (mag., v.4, #4): Phantasm Press, Fall 1986.
-   (c) *City Fishing* (f.c.): Silver Salamander Press, 2000.

"Black"
-   (1) *After Hours* (mag., #3): William G. Raley, Summer 1989.
-   (c) *Out of the Dark: A Storybook of Horrors* (f.c.): Centipede Press, 2016.

"Blattidae Wine"
-   (1) *Weird Fiction Review* (mag., #7): Centipede Press, Fall 2016.

"Blood Knot"
-   (1) *Forbidden Acts* (anth., ed. Nancy Collins): Avon, 1995.
-   (r) *The Year's Best Fantasy and Horror: Ninth Annual Collection* (anth., ed. Ellen Datlow and Terri Windling): St. Martin's Griffin, 1996.
-   (c) *Ugly Behavior* (f.c.): New Pulp Press, 2012.

"**B**loodwolf" (NOTE: Story later revised, became a chapter in the novel, *Deadfall Hotel*).

(1) *Shadows* 9 (anth., ed. Charles L. Grant): Doubleday, 1986.

"**B**lue Alice"

(1) *The Dedalus Book of Femmes Fatales* (anth., ed. Brian Stableford): Dedalus, 1992.

(c) *Out of the Dark: A Storybook of Horrors* (f.c.): Centipede Press, 2016.

"**B**odies and Heads"

(1) *Book of the Dead* (anth., ed. John Skipp and Craig Spector): Bantam, 1989.

(r) *Zombies: Encounters with the Hungry Dead* (anth., ed. John Skipp): Black Dog & Leventhal, 2009.

(r) *Zombie! Zombie! Zombie!* (anth., ed. Otto Penzler): Vintage Crime/ Black Lizard/ Vintage Books, 2011.

(c) *Out of the Dark: A Storybook of Horrors* (f.c.): Centipede Press, 2016.

"**B**ouquet"

(1) *Absences: Charlie Goode's Ghosts—Haunted Library "Psychic Sleuths' Booklet Number Two"* (chapbook including 6 stories): Haunted Library, 1991.

(c) *The Far Side of the Lake* (f.c.): Ash-Tree Press, 2001.

"**B**oxer"

(1) *New Blood* (mag., #4): Chris B. Lacher, Fall 1988.

(r) *Splatterpunks II: Over the Edge* (anth., ed. Paul Sammon): Tor, 1995.

(c) *City Fishing* (f.c.): Silver Salamander Press, 2000.

"**B**oy Blue"

(1) *Weird Tales #2* (anth., ed. Lin Carter): Zebra Books/ Kensington Publishing Corp., Spring 1981.

"The **B**oyfriend"

(1) *Scary Out There* (anth., ed. Jonathan Maberry): Simon &

Schuster, 2016.

"**B**rain of Shadows"
(1) *Psychos* (anth., ed. Michael Arnzen): Mastication Publications, 1992.
(r) *The 1993 Rhysling Anthology: The Best Science Fiction, Fantasy and Horror Poetry of 1992* (anth., ed. J. C. Hendee and Barb Hendee): SFPA, 1993.
(c) *Onion Songs* (f.c.): Chomu Press, 2013.

"**B**reaking the Rules"
(1) *Narrow Houses* (anth., ed. Peter Crowther): Little, Brown UK, 1992.
(c) *Here With the Shadows* (f.c.): Swan River Press, 2014.

"**B**reathing"
(1) *Black Static* (mag., #53): TTA Press, Aug./Sept. 2016.

"The **B**rollachan"
(1) *Nightmares Unhinged: Twenty Tales of Terror* (anth., ed. Joshua Viola): Hex Publishers, 2015.

"**B**rooms Welcome the Dust"
(1) *The Ultimate Witch* (anth., ed. John Gregory Betancourt and Byron Preiss): Byron Preiss Visual Publications, 1993.
(c) *City Fishing* (f.c.): Silver Salamander Press, 2000.

"**B**rutes"
(1) *Iniquities* (mag., #3): Iniquities Publications, Autumn 1991.
(c) *City Fishing* (f.c.): Silver Salamander Press, 2000.

"The **B**urdens"
(1) *Dante's Disciples* (anth., ed. Peter Crowther and Edward E. Kramer): Borealis/ White Wolf Publishing, 1995.
(c) *City Fishing* (f.c.): Silver Salamander Press, 2000.

"**B**urning Snow"
(1) *Exotic Gothic 2: New Tales of Taboo* (anth., ed. Danel Olson): Ash-Tree Press, 2008.

(c) *Out of the Dark: A Storybook of Horrors* (f.c.): Centipede Press, 2016.

"Buzz"

(1) *Mile High Futures* (mag., v.3, #11): Mile High Comics, Nov. 1985.

(r) *Isaac Asimov's Science Fiction Magazine* (mag., v.10, #12): Davis Publications, Dec. 1986.

(c) *City Fishing* (f.c.): Silver Salamander Press, 2000.

"The Cabinet Child"

(1) *Phantom* (anth., ed. Paul Tremblay and Sean Wallace): Prime Books, 2008.

(r) *The Year's Best Dark Fantasy & Horror 2010 Edition* (anth., ed. Paula Guran): Prime Books, 2010.

(c) *Here With the Shadows* (f.c.): Swan River Press, 2014.

"Cannondale at the Beach"

(c) *Out of the Dark: A Storybook of Horrors* (f.c.): Centipede Press, 2016.

"The Carl Paradox"

(1) *Asimov's Science Fiction* (mag., v.38, #1): Dell Magazines, Jan. 2014.

"Carnal House"

(1) *Hot Blood 1: Tales of Provocative Horror* (anth., ed. Jeff Gelb and Lonn Friend): Pocket Books, 1989.

(r) *The Mammoth Book of Best New Horror, Vol. 1* (anth., ed. Stephen Jones and Ramsey Campbell): Carroll & Graf, 1990.

(r) *The Giant Book of Best New Horror* (anth., ed. Stephen Jones and Ramsey Campbell): Magpie Books, 1993.

(c) *City Fishing* (f.c.): Silver Salamander Press, 2000.

"The Carving"

(1) *Argosy Quarterly* (mag., #3): Coppervale International, Sept. 2005.

(c) *Ugly Behavior* (f.c.): New Pulp Press, 2012.

"A Cascade of Lies"
(1) *David Copperfield's Beyond Imagination* (anth., ed. David Copperfield and Janet Berliner): HarperPrism, 1996.
(c) *Out of the Dark: A Storybook of Horrors* (f.c.): Centipede Press, 2016.

"Cats, Dogs, and Other Creatures"
(1) *Talebones* (mag., #21): Fairwood Press, Spring 2001.
(r) *The Best of Talebones* (anth., ed. Patrick Swenson): Fairwood Press, 2010.
(c) *Onion Songs* (f.c.): Chomu Press, 2013.

"Cattiwampus"
(1) *The Devil's Coattails* (anth., ed. Jason V Brock and William Nolan): Cycatrix Press, 2011.
(c) *Out of the Dark: A Storybook of Horrors* (f.c.): Centipede Press, 2016.

"Celestial Inventory"
(1) (chapbook): Chris Drumm (Drumm Booklet), 1991.
(c) *Celestial Inventories* (f.c.): ChiZine Publications, 2013.

"Chain Reaction"
(1) *Black Static* (mag., #19): TTA Press, Oct./Nov. 2010.
(c) *Celestial Inventories* (f.c.): ChiZine Publications, 2013.

"The Changing Room"
(c) *Onion Songs* (f.c.): Chomu Press, 2013.

"Charles"
(1) *Black Static* (mag., #12): TTA Press, Aug./Sept. 2009.
(r) *Dark Light* (anth., ed. Carl Hose): MARLvision Publishing, 2012.
(c) *Onion Songs* (f.c.): Chomu Press, 2013.

"The Child Killer"
(1) *Monsters In Our Midst (anth., ed.* Robert Bloch): Tor, 1993.
(c) *Ugly Behavior* (f.c.): New Pulp Press, 2012.

"City Fishing"

> (1) *New Terrors 1* (anth., ed. Ramsey Campbell): Pan Books, 1980.
>
> (r) *New Terrors Omnibus* (anth., ed. Ramsey Campbell): Pan Books, 1985.
>
> (c) *City Fishing* (f.c.): Silver Salamander Press, 2000.

"Close to You"

> (1) *Bones of the Children* (mag., #1): CFD Publications, Fall 1996.
>
> (r) *Obsession: Tales of Irresistible Desire* (anth., ed. Paula Guran): Prime Books, 2012.

"Cold & Damp"

> (1) *Great Jones Street* (online app): greatjonesstreet.press, Feb. 2017.

"A Common Sea"

> (1) *Interzone* (mag., #269): TTA Press, Mar./Apr. 2017.

"The Company You Keep"

> (1) *Outsiders: 22 All-New Stories from the Edge* (anth., ed. Nancy Holder and Nancy Kilpatrick): Roc/ New American Library, 2005.
>
> (c) *Celestial Inventories* (f.c.): ChiZine Publications, 2013.

"Congregate"

> (1) *Lore* (mag., v.2, #2): The LORE Firm, Nov. 2012
>
> (c) *Out of the Dark: A Storybook of Horrors* (f.c.): Centipede Press, 2016.

"Cornwoman"

> (1) *Dragon Magazine* (mag., #145): TSR, Inc. (Dragon Publishing), May 1989.

"The Cough"

> (1) *Horrors! 365 Scary Stories* (anth., ed. Stefan R. Dziemianowicz, Robert H. Weinberg, and Martin H. Greenberg): Barnes & Noble Books, 1998.
>
> (c) *Ugly Behavior* (f.c.): New Pulp Press, 2012.

"Crawldaddies"
  (1) *Searchers After Horror: New Tales of the Weird and Fantastic* (anth., ed. S.T. Joshi): Fedogan & Bremer, 2014.

"Creation Story"
  (1) *Otherworldly Maine* (anth., ed. Noreen Doyle): Down East Books, 2008.

"Creeps"
  (1) *Embraces: Dark Erotica* (anth., ed. Paula Guran): Venus or Vixen Press, 2000.

"The Crusher"
  (1) *Crimewave 6: Breaking Point* (anth., ed. Andy Cox): TTA Press, 2002.
  (c) *Ugly Behavior* (f.c.): New Pulp Press, 2012.

"Crutches"
  (1) *Shadows 6* (anth., ed. Charles L. Grant): Doubleday, 1983.
  (r) *100 Twisted Little Tales of Torment* (anth., ed. Stefan R. Dziemianowicz, Robert H. Weinberg, and Martin H. Greenberg): Barnes & Noble Books, 1998.
  (c) *The Far Side of the Lake* (f.c.): Ash-Tree Press, 2001.

"Cubs"
  (1) *Hideous Progeny* (anth., ed. Brian Willis): RazorBlade Press, 2000.
  (c) *Twember: Science Fiction Stories; Imaginings vol. 7* (f.c.): NewCon Press, 2013.

"Cutlery"
  (1) *Absences: Charlie Goode's Ghosts—Haunted Library "Psychic Sleuths' Booklet Number Two"* (chapbook including 6 stories): Haunted Library, 1991.
  (c) *The Far Side of the Lake* (f.c.): Ash-Tree Press, 2001.

"Daddy"
  (1) *Footsteps* (mag., #7): Bill Munster, Nov. 1986.

(r) *100 Ghastly Little Ghost Stories* (anth., ed. Stefan R. Dziemianowicz, Robert H. Weinberg, and Martin H. Greenberg): Barnes & Noble Books, 1993.

(r) *Smithereens: A Collection of Short Short Stories* (anth., ed. Richard Baines; Australian school text): Oxford University Press, 1998.

"Daddy's An Actor"
(1) *New Mystery* (mag., #1): New Mystery, July/ Aug. 1991.

"Dancers In The Leaves"
(1) *All Hallows* (mag., #2): The Ghost Story Society, 1990.
(c) *The Far Side of the Lake* (f.c.): Ash-Tree Press, 2001.

"Dark Shapes in the Road"
(1) *Night Visions 1* (anth., ed. Alan Ryan): Dark Harvest, 1984.
(r) *Night Visions: In the Blood* (anth., ed. Alan Ryan): Berkley Books, 1988.
(r) *Dark Dreams* (mag., #6): Dark Dreams, 1988.
(c) *The Far Side of the Lake* (f.c.): Ash-Tree Press, 2001.

"The Day Before the Day Before"
(1) *Asimov's Science Fiction* (mag., v.33, #9): Dell Magazines, Sept. 2009.
(c) *Twember: Science Fiction Stories; Imaginings vol. 7* (f.c.): NewCon Press, 2013.

"The Day It Rained Vaginas"
(1) *Last Wave* (mag., v.1, #3): Last Wave, Summer 1984.

"Daytimer"
(1) *Horrors! 365 Scary Stories* (anth., ed. Stefan R. Dziemianowicz, Robert H. Weinberg, and Martin H. Greenberg): Barnes & Noble Books, 1998.

"December"
(1) *Horrors! 365 Scary Stories* (anth., ed. Stefan R. Dziemianowicz, Robert H. Weinberg, and Martin H. Greenberg): Barnes & Noble Books, 1998.

(c) *Onion Songs* (f.c.): Chomu Press, 2013.

"Decodings"

    (c) *Decoded Mirrors: 3 Tales After Lovecraft* (chapbook including 3 stories): Necronomicon Press, 1992.

    (c) *The Far Side of the Lake* (f.c.): Ash-Tree Press, 2001.

"The Deep Blue Sea"

    (1) *New Blood* (mag., #5): Chris B. Lacher, Winter 1989.

"Deep Fracture"

    (1) *Madness of Cthulhu Volume 2* (anth., ed. S. T. Joshi): Titan Books, 2015.

"Denegare Spasticus"

    (1) *The Thackery T. Lambshead Pocket Guide to Eccentric & Discredited Diseases* (anth., ed. Jeff Vandermeer and Mark Roberts): Night Shade Books, 2003.

"Derangement"

    (c) *City Fishing* (f.c.): Silver Salamander Press, 2000.

"Derelicts"

    The Dodd, Mead Gallery of Horror (anth., ed. Charles L. Grant): Dodd, Mead, 1983.

    (c) *The Far Side of the Lake* (f.c.): Ash-Tree Press, 2001.

"Dinosaur"

    (1) *Isaac Asimov's Science Fiction Magazine* (mag., v.11, #5): Davis Publications, May 1987.

    (r) *Dinosaurs!* (anth., ed. Jack Dann and Gardner Dozois): Ace Books, 1990.

    (r) *Where Past Meets Present: Modern Colorado Short Stories* (anth., ed. James B. Hemesath): Univ Pr of Colorado, 1994.

    (c) *Celestial Inventories* (f.c.): ChiZine Publications, 2013.

"The Disease Artist"

    (1) *Dark Arts* (anth., ed. John Pelan): Cemetery Dance Publications, 2006.

(c) *Celestial Inventories* (f.c.): ChiZine Publications, 2013.

"Disturb Not Her Dream"
>   (1) *The Ultimate Silver Surfer* (anth., ed. Stan Lee): Boulevard Books, 1995.

"Does It Scare You?"
>   (1) *Gorezone* (mag., #8): O'Quinn Studios, July 1989.

"The Doll Thief"
>   (1) *The Third Alternative* (mag., #17): TTA Press, 1998.
>   (c) *Out of the Dark: A Storybook of Horrors* (f.c.): Centipede Press, 2016.

"Domestic Magic" (with Melanie Tem)
>   (1) *Magic, An Anthology of the Esoteric and Arcane* (anth., ed. Jon Oliver): Solaris, 2012.
>   (r) *The Best Science Fiction and Fantasy of the Year: Volume Seven* (anth., ed. Jonathan Strahan): Night Shade Books, 2013.

"Doodles"
>   (1) *Sinistre: An Anthology of Rituals* (anth., ed. George Hatch): Horror's Head Press, 1993.
>   (r) *The Year's Best Fantasy and Horror: Seventh Annual Collection* (anth., ed. Ellen Datlow and Terri Windling): St. Martin's Griffin, 1994.
>   (c) *Onion Songs* (f.c.): Chomu Press, 2013.

"The Doors of Hypertext"
>   (1) *Infinite Loop: Stories About the Future by the People Creating It* (anth., ed. Larry Constantine): Miller Freeman, 1993.

"A Dream of the Dead"
>   (1) *Album Zutique* (anth., ed. Jeff Vandermeer): Night Shade Books, 2003.
>   (c) *Onion Songs* (f.c.): Chomu Press, 2013.

"The Drowned Man"
>   (c) *Out of the Dark: A Storybook of Horrors* (f.c.): Centipede Press, 2016.

"Dune Shack"
> (1) *New Frontiers, Volume II* (anth., ed. Bill Pronzini and Martin H. Greenberg): Tor, 1990.

"The Dying"
> (1) *Jabberwocky* (fanzine, #2): Chimera Connections, Inc., Spring/Summer 1992.

"Dying on the Elephant Road"
> (1) *Beneath Ceaseless Skies* (e-mag., #54): Beneath Ceaseless Skies, Oct. 2010.

"Each Day"
> (1) *Horrors! 365 Scary Stories* (anth., ed. Stefan R. Dziemianowicz, Robert H. Weinberg, and Martin H. Greenberg): Barnes & Noble Books, 1998.
> (c) *Out of the Dark: A Storybook of Horrors* (f.c.): Centipede Press, 2016.

"Early Warning"
> (1) *Owlflight* (mag., #2): Millea Kenin, 1981.

"Eddie the Great"
> (1) *The Monkey's Other Paw* (anth., ed. Luis Ortiz): Nonstop Press, 2014.

"Eggs"
> (c) *City Fishing* (f.c.): Silver Salamander Press, 2000.
> (r) *Weird Shadows over Innsmouth* (anth., ed. Stephen Jones): Fedogan & Bremer, 2005.

"Elena"
> (1) *Darkside: Horror for the Next Millennium* (anth., ed. John Pelan): Darkside Press, 1996.
> (c) *Out of the Dark: A Storybook of Horrors* (f.c.): Centipede Press, 2016.

"El Lagarto"
> (1) *More Tales of Zorro* (anth., ed. Richard Dean Starr): Moonstone, 2011.

"Embrace of Clay, Embrace of Straw"
> (1) *Crypt of Cthulhu* (fanzine, #39): Cryptic Publications, 1986.

"Empty Morning" (with Melanie Tem)
> (1) *The Many Faces of Van Helsing* (anth., ed. Jeanne Cavelos): Ace books, 2004.
>
> (c) *In Concert* (with Melanie Tem) (collection of collaborations): Centipede Press, 2010.

"End of the Yarn"
> (1) *Weirdbook* (mag., #19): W. Paul Ganley, 1984.
>
> (c) *Out of the Dark: A Storybook of Horrors* (f.c.): Centipede Press, 2016.

"An Ending"
> (1) *A Walk On the Darkside: Visions of Horror* (anth., ed. John Pelan): Roc/ New American Library, 2004.
>
> (c) *Onion Songs* (f.c.): Chomu Press, 2013.

"The Enemy Within"
> (1) *Something Remains—Joel Lane & Friends* (anth., ed. Peter Coleborn and Pauline E. Dungate): Alchemy Press, 2016.

"The Enormous Lover"
> (1) *Last Wave* (mag., #1): Scott Edelman, Oct. 1983.

"Ephemera"
> (1) *Asimov's Science Fiction* (mag., v.35, #12): Dell Magazines, Dec. 2011.
>
> (c) *Twember: Science Fiction Stories; Imaginings vol. 7* (f.c.): NewCon Press, 2013.

"The Erased"
> (1) *Shadows & Tall Trees 7* (anth., ed. Michael Kelly): Undertow Publications, 2017.

"Escape on a Train"
> (1) *Pulphouse: The Hardback Magazine* (mag., #7): Pulphouse Publishing, Spring 1990.

(r) *Rustblind and Silverbright—A Slipstream Anthology of Railway Stories* (anth., ed. David Rix): Eibonvale Press, 2013.

(c) *The Far Side of the Lake* (f.c.): Ash-Tree Press, 2001.

"Espectare Necrosis"

(1) *The Thackery T. Lambshead Pocket Guide to Eccentric & Discredited Diseases* (anth., ed. Jeff Vandermeer and Mark Roberts): Night Shade Books, 2003.

"Est Enim Magnum Chaos"

(1) *Sorcery and Sanctity: A Homage to Arthur Machen* (anth., ed. Daniel Corrick): Hieroglyphic Press, 2013.

(c) *Here With the Shadows (f.c.): Swan River Press, 2014.*

"The Ex"

(1) *Box of Delights* (anth., ed. John Kenny): Aeon Press, 2011.

(r) Ghosts: Recent Hauntings (anth., ed. Paula Guran): Prime Books, 2012.

(c) *Out of the Dark: A Storybook of Horrors* (f.c.): Centipede Press, 2016.

"Excavation"

(1) (short story version with the novel), *Excavation* (hard cover edition, Dark Essential Series): Delirium Books, 2006.

"Facing It"

(1) *Mike Shayne Mystery Magazine* (mag., v.48, #4): Renown Publications, Inc., Apr. 1984.

"A Fairytale"

(1) *Pig Iron: Science Fiction* (anth., #10 in a series, ed. Rose Sayre and Jim Villani): Pig Iron Press, 1982.

"Fairytales"

(1) (chapbook): Roadkill Press, 1990.

(r) *Pulphouse: The Hardback Magazine* (mag., #12): Pulphouse Publishing, Fall 1993.

(c) *City Fishing* (f.c.): Silver Salamander Press, 2000.

"Family"
> (1) *Andrew Vachss' Underground #1* (anth./ comic, ed. Neal Barrett, Jr. and Jerry Prosser): Dark Horse Comics, 1993.
> (c) *Out of the Dark: A Storybook of Horrors* (f.c.): Centipede Press, 2016.

"The Farmer"
> (1) *The 16th Fontana Book of Great Horror Stories* (anth., ed. Mary Danby): Fontana, 1983.

"*The Far Side of the Lake*"
> (c) *The Far Side of the Lake* (f.c.): Ash-Tree Press, 2001.

"Father's Day"
> (1) *Whispers* V (anth., ed. Stuart David Schiff): Doubleday, 1985.
> (c) *City Fishing* (f.c.): Silver Salamander Press, 2000.

"The Figure In Motion"
> (1) *The Company He Keeps (Postscripts 22/23)* (anth., ed. Peter Crowther and Nick Gevers): PS Publishing, 2010.
> (c) *Onion Songs* (f.c.): Chomu Press, 2013.

"Filmmaker"
> (1) *Chrysalis* 8 (anth., ed. Roy Torgeson): Doubleday, 1980.

"Final Apprentice"
> (1) *Betcha Can't Read Just One* (anth., ed. Alan Dean Foster): Ace Books (Ace Fantasy), 1993.
> (r) *100 Little Humorous Stories* (anth., ed. Stefan R. Dziemianowicz, Robert H. Weinberg, and Martin H. Greenberg): Barnes & Noble Books, 1999.

"Firestorm"
> (1) *Perpetual Light* (anth., ed. Alan Ryan): Warner Books, 1982.
> (c) *Celestial Inventories* (f.c.): ChiZine Publications, 2013.

"First Rights"
> (1) *Space and Time (mag., #65)*: Gordon Linzner, Winter 1983.

"Fish"

(1) *Horror D'oeuvres* (DarkFuse Magazine) (online media): darkfusemagazine.com, 2006.

(c) *Onion Songs* (f.c.): Chomu Press, 2013.

"The Fishing Hut"

(1) *Black Static* (mag., #45): TTA Press, Mar./ Apr. 2015.

"Fogwell"

(1) *Doom City (Greystone Bay Chronicle 2* (anth., ed. Charles L. Grant): Tor, 1987.

(c) *The Far Side of the Lake* (f.c.): Ash-Tree Press, 2001.

"Forty-three Thousand Sunsets"

(c) *Twember: Science Fiction Stories; Imaginings vol. 7* (f.c.): NewCon Press, 2013.

"Forward"

(1) *Destinies* (anth., ed. Jim Baen): Ace Books, Feb./Mar. 1980.

(r) *A Spadeful of Spacetime* (anth., ed. Fred Saberhagen): Ace Books, 1981.

(c) *Twember: Science Fiction Stories; Imaginings vol. 7* (f.c.): NewCon Press, 2013.

"Frank at 26"

(1) *Thin Air Wonder Stories* (mag., #1): Denvention Two Inc., 1979.

"Friday Nights"

(1) *Crimewave 8: Cold Harbours* (anth., ed. Andy Cox): TTA Press, 2005.

(c) *Ugly Behavior* (f.c.): New Pulp Press, 2012.

"G is for Ghost"

(c) *Here With the Shadows* (f.c.): Swan River Press, 2014.

"Garbage"

(1) *In Delirium 2* (anth., ed. John Everson): Delirium Books, 2006.

"The Garden, In Autumn"

   (1) *Deathrealm* (mag., #22): TAL Publications, Summer 1994.

"Ghost in the Machine"

   (1) *Bloodsongs* (mag., #7): Bambada Press, 1996.

   (r) *The Mammoth Book of Best New Horror, Vol. 8* (anth., ed. Stephen Jones): Carroll & Graf/ Running Press, 1997.

   (c) *City Fishing* (f.c.): Silver Salamander Press, 2000.

"Giant Killers"

   (1) *Pedestal* (e-mag., #61): thepedestalmagazine.com, Dec. 2010.

   (c) *Celestial Inventories* (f.c.): ChiZine Publications, 2013.

"The Giveaway"

   (1) *Shadows* 4 (anth., ed. Charles L. Grant): Doubleday, 1981.

   (r) *100 Great Fantasy Short Short Stories* (anth., ed. by Isaac Asimov, Terry Carr, and Martin H. Greenberg): Avon, 1984.

   (r) *100 Hair-raising Little Horror Stories* (anth., ed. Al Sarrantonio and Martin H. Greenberg): Barnes & Noble Books, 1993.

   (r) *Horror from the Inside Out: Authors for Autism* (anth., ed. Lisa Dabrowski): Whorror House, 2016.

   (c) *Out of the Dark: A Storybook of Horrors* (f.c.): Centipede Press, 2016.

   (c) *Exploring Dark Short Fiction #1: A Primer to Steve Rasnic Tem* (f.c., ed. Eric J. Guignard): Dark Moon Books, 2017.

"The Glare and the Glow"

   (1) *Interzone* (mag., #227): TTA Press, Mar./ Apr. 2010.

   (c) *Onion Songs* (f.c.): Chomu Press, 2013.

"Going North"

   (1) *Northern Frights 1* (anth., ed. Don Hutchinson): Mosaic Press, 1992.

   (c) *Out of the Dark: A Storybook of Horrors* (f.c.): Centipede Press, 2016.

"Goode Farm"

   (1) *Absences: Charlie Goode's Ghosts—Haunted Library "Psychic*

Sleuths' Booklet Number Two" (chapbook including 6 stories): Haunted Library, 1991.

   (c) *The Far Side of the Lake* (f.c.): Ash-Tree Press, 2001.

"Grandfather Wolf"

   (1) *Werewolves & Shapeshifters* (anth., ed. John Skipp): Black Dog & Leventhal, 2010.

   (c) *Out of the Dark: A Storybook of Horrors* (f.c.): Centipede Press, 2016.

"The Grave House"

   (1) *Strange Tales V* (anth., ed. Rosalie Parker): Tartarus Press, 2015.

"The Green Dog"

   (1) *Null Immortalis: Nemonymous 10* (anth., ed. D.F. Lewis): Megazanthus Press, 2010.

   (c) *Onion Songs* (f.c.): Chomu Press, 2013.

"Grim Monkeys"

   (1) *Tropical Chills*, Avon (anth., ed. Tim Sullivan): Avon, 1988.

   (c) *The Far Side of the Lake* (f.c.): Ash-Tree Press, 2001.

"Guardian Angels"

   (1) *Decoded Mirrors: 3 Tales After Lovecraft* (chapbook including 3 stories): Necronomicon Press, 1992

   (c) *Out of the Dark: A Storybook of Horrors* (f.c.): Centipede Press, 2016.

"Half-Light"

   (1) *Uncertainties: Vol 2* (anth., ed. Brian Showers): The Swan River Press, 2016.

"Halloween Street"

   (1) *The Magazine of Fantasy & Science Fiction* (digest, v.97, #1): Mercury Press, July 1999.

   (r) *The Year's Best Fantasy & Horror: Thirteenth Annual Collection* (anth., ed. Ellen Datlow and Terri Windling): St. Martin's Griffin, 2000.

(r) *The Mammoth Book of Best New Horror, Vol. 11* (anth., ed. Stephen Jones): Carroll & Graf/ Running Press, 2000.

(r) *Halloween* (anth., ed. Paula Guran): Prime Books, 2011.

(c) *Celestial Inventories* (f.c.): ChiZine Publications, 2013.

"The Hanged Man"
(1) *Black Static* (mag., #40): TTA Press, May/ June 2014.

"Harvest Child"
(1) *Elsewhere, Vol. III* (anth., ed. Terri Windling and Mark Alan Arnold): Ace Books, 1984.

(r) *The Year's Best Fantasy Stories 11* (anth., ed. Arthur W. Saha): DAW Books, 1985.

"Head Explosions"
(1) *Bust Down the Door and Eat All the Chickens* (journal, v.2, #5): No Girls Allowed Press, 2006.

(c) *Celestial Inventories* (f.c.): ChiZine Publications, 2013.

"Hearts"
(1) *Absences: Charlie Goode's Ghosts—Haunted Library "Psychic Sleuths' Booklet Number Two"* (chapbook including 6 stories): Haunted Library, 1991.

(c) *The Far Side of the Lake* (f.c.): Ash-Tree Press, 2001.

"Heat"
(1) *White of the Moon: New Tales of Madness and Dread* (anth., ed. Stephen Jones): Pumpkin Books, 1999.

(r) *The Year's Best Fantasy & Horror: Thirteenth Annual Collection* (anth., ed. Ellen Datlow and Terri Windling): St. Martin's Griffin, 2000.

(r) *Darkness: Two Decades of Modern Horror* (anth., ed. Ellen Datlow):
Tachyon Publications, 2010.

(c) *Out of the Dark: A Storybook of Horrors* (f.c.): Centipede Press, 2016.

"Her New Parents"
(1) *Weirdbook* (mag., #23/24): W. Paul Ganley, 1988.
(r) *100 Ghastly Little Ghost Stories* (anth., ed. Stefan R. Dziemianowicz, Robert H. Weinberg, and Martin H. Greenberg): Barnes & Noble Books, 1993.

"Her Oh So Pretty Face"
(1) *Words* (online media): hexpublishers.com, Jan. 2017.

"Here With the Shadows"
(c) *Here With the Shadows* (f.c.): Swan River Press, 2014.
(r) *Better Weird: A Tribute to David B. Silva* (anth., ed. Richard Chizmar, Brian Freeman, Paul F. Olson): Cemetery Dance Publications, 2016.

"The Hideaway Man"
(1) *A Nightmare's Dozen* (anth., ed. Michael Stearns): HMH Books for Young Readers, 1996.

"Hideout"
(1) *Other Worlds 1* (anth., ed. Roy Torgeson): Zebra Books/ Kensington Publishing Corp, 1979.

"Hidey Hole"
(1) *Masques II* (anth., ed. J.N. Williamson): Maclay & Associates, 1987.
(r) *The Best of Masques* (anth., ed. J.N. Williamson): Berkley Books, 1988.
(c) *City Fishing* (f.c.): Silver Salamander Press, 2000.

"The High Chair"
(1) *Fly Trap* (mag., #6): Tropism Press, 2006.
(c) *Celestial Inventories* (f.c.): ChiZine Publications, 2013.

"The Hijacker"
(1) *Eldritch Tales* (mag., #8): Yith Press, 1982.
(c) *Onion Songs* (f.c.): Chomu Press, 2013.

"Hooks"
- (1) *Fear* (mag., #5): Newsfield Publications Ltd, Mar./Apr. 1989.
- (c) *City Fishing* (f.c.): Silver Salamander Press, 2000.

"The House by the Bulvarnoye Koltso"
- (1) *Exotic Gothic: Forbidden Tales From Our Gothic World* (anth., ed. Danel Olson): Ash-Tree Press, 2007.
- (c) *Out of the Dark: A Storybook of Horrors* (f.c.): Centipede Press, 2016.

"A House by the Ocean"
- (c) *Here With the Shadows* (f.c.): Swan River Press, 2014.

"Houses Creaking in the Wind"
- (1) *Horrors! 365 Scary Stories* (anth., ed. Stefan R. Dziemianowicz, Robert H. Weinberg, and Martin H. Greenberg): Barnes & Noble Books, 1998.
- (c) *The Far Side of the Lake* (f.c.): Ash-Tree Press, 2001.

"Housewarming"
- (1) *The 18th Fontana Book of Great Ghost Stories* (anth., ed. R. Chetwynd Hayes): Fontana, 1982.
- (r) *Great Ghost Stories* (anth., ed. R. Chetwynd Hayes and Stephen Jones): Carroll & Graf, 2004.
- (c) *Out of the Dark: A Storybook of Horrors* (f.c.): Centipede Press, 2016.

"How To Survive a Fire at the Greenmark" (written as Astrid Halsey)
- (1) *The Spook: April Fools Issue* (mag., #9): thespook.com, Apr./May 2002.
- (r) *Tales From the Crossroad Volume One* (anth., ed. David Niall Wilson and David Dodd): Crossroad Press, 2011.
- (c) *Onion Songs* (f.c.): Chomu Press, 2013.

"A Hundred Wicked Little Witches, A"
- (1) *100 Wicked Little Witch Stories* (anth., ed. Stefan R. Dziemianowicz, Robert H. Weinberg, and Martin H. Greenberg): Barnes & Noble Books, 1995.

(r) *The Mammoth Book of Best New Horror, Vol. 7* (anth., ed. Stephen Jones): Carroll & Graf/ Running Press, 1996.

(c) *City Fishing* (f.c.): Silver Salamander Press, 2000.

(c) *Out of the Dark: A Storybook of Horrors* (f.c.): Centipede Press, 2016.

"Hungry"

(1) *Borderlands* 3 (anth., ed. Tom Monteleone): Borderlands Press, 1992.

(r) *The Year's Best Fantasy and Horror: Sixth Annual Collection* (anth., ed. Ellen Datlow and Terri Windling): St. Martin's Griffin, 1993.

(c) *City Fishing* (f.c.): Silver Salamander Press, 2000.

(c) *Exploring Dark Short Fiction #1: A Primer to Steve Rasnic Tem* (f.c., ed. Eric J. Guignard): Dark Moon Books, 2017.

"The Hunt"

(1) *Dead of Night* (mag., #8): Dead of Night, Fall/Winter 1993.

"The Hunter Home From the Hill"

(1) *2001 (unknown periodical* in India): *unknown publisher*, July 1991.

(c) *Onion Songs* (f.c.): Chomu Press, 2013.

"Ice House Pond"

(1) *In The Fog (Greystone Bay Chronicle 4)* (anth., ed. Charles L. Grant): Tor, 1993.

(r) *The Mammoth Book of Best New Horror, Vol. 5* (anth., ed. Stephen Jones and Ramsey Campbell): Carroll & Graf, 1994.

(c) *The Far Side of the Lake* (f.c.): Ash-Tree Press, 2001.

"In a Guest House"

(1) *Greystone Bay (Greystone Bay Chronicle 1* (anth., ed. Charles L. Grant): Tor, 1985.

(c) *The Far Side of the Lake* (f.c.): Ash-Tree Press, 2001.

"In All Things Moderation"

(1) *Fantasy Book* (fanzine, #2): Fantasy Book Enterprises, Dec. 1981.

"In Concert" (with Melanie Tem)

(1) *Asimov's Science Fiction* (mag., v.32, #12): Dell Magazines, Dec. 2008

(c) *In Concert* (with Melanie Tem) (collection of collaborations): Centipede Press, 2010.

"In Control"

(1) *Tales as Like as Not* (fanzine, #9): Second Unit Productions, Winter 1986.

"In His Image"

(1) *Crimewave 2: Deepest Red* (anth., ed. Andy Cox): TTA Press, 1999.

(c) *Ugly Behavior* (f.c.): New Pulp Press, 2012.

"In the Lovecraft Museum"

(1) (novella): PS Publishing, 2015.

(r) *The Mammoth Book of Best New Horror, Vol. 27* (anth., ed. Stephen Jones): Carroll & Graf/ Running Press, 2017.

"In the Trees"

(1) *Fantasy Tales* (mag., v.11, #4): Robinson, Spring 1990.

(r) *New Masterpieces of Horror* (anth., ed. John Betancourt): Barnes & Noble Books, 1996.

(r) *The Year's Best Fantasy and Horror: Fourth Annual Collection* (anth., ed. Ellen Datlow and Terri Windling): St. Martin's Griffin, 1991.

(r) *The Giant Book of Fantasy Tales* (anth., ed. Stephen Jones and David Sutton): The Book Company, 1996.

(r) *Horrorscape: New Masterpieces of Horror, Vol. 1* (anth., ed. John Betancourt): ibooks, 2005.

(c) *The Far Side of the Lake* (f.c.): Ash-Tree Press, 2001.

"In These Final Days of Sales"

(1) (chapbook): Wormhole Books, 2001.

(r) *The Year's Best Fantasy & Horror: Fifteenth Annual Collection* (anth., ed. Ellen Datlow and Terri Windling): St. Martin's

Griffin, 2002.

(c) *Celestial Inventories* (f.c.): ChiZine Publications, 2013.

(c) *Exploring Dark Short Fiction #1: A Primer to Steve Rasnic Tem* (f.c., ed. Eric J. Guignard): Dark Moon Books, 2017.

"Inside William James"

(1) *Acquainted With The Night* (anth., ed. Barbara Roden and Christopher Roden, 2004.

(c) *Here With the Shadows* (f.c.): Swan River Press, 2014.

"Interlude in a Laboratory"

(1) *Isaac Asimov's Science Fiction Magazine* (mag., v.5, #8): Davis Publications, Aug. 1981.

(r) *100 Humorous Little Stories* (anth., ed. Stefan R. Dziemianowicz, Robert H. Weinberg, and Martin H. Greenberg): Barnes & Noble Books, 1999.

"Invisible"

(1) *Sci-Fi.com*, Mar. 2005.

(r) *Fantasy, The Best of the Year* 2006 (anth., ed. Rich Horton.

(c) *Celestial Inventories* (f.c.): ChiZine Publications, 2013.

"Jack and Jill"

(1) *Screaming Book of Horror* (anth., ed. Johnny Mains): Screaming Dreams, 2012.

(c) *Out of the Dark: A Storybook of Horrors* (f.c.): Centipede Press, 2016.

"Jake's Body"

(1) *Be Afraid!* (anth., ed. Edo van Belkom): Tundra Books, 2000.

"Janael"

(1) *Pirate Writings* (mag., #8): Pirate Writings Publishing, 1995.

"Jason's Nightmare"

(1) *The Ultimate Super-Villains* (anth., ed. Stan Lee): Boulevard Books, 1996.

"Jesse"

(1) *Psycho-Paths* (anth., ed. Robert Bloch): Tor, 1991.

(r) *Psychos* (anth., ed. John Skipp): Black Dog & Leventhal, 2012.

(c) *Ugly Behavior* (f.c.): New Pulp Press, 2012.

"Jungle J.D."

(1) *It Came From the Drive-in* (anth., ed. Norman Partridge): DAW Books, 1996.

(c) *Onion Songs* (f.c.): Chomu Press, 2013.

"Katherine's Shadow"

(1) *Borderland* (mag., #4): Artimus Publications, 1986.

"Kiss"

(1) *Dark Horizons* (mag., #24): The British Fantasy Society, Winter 1981.

"Kite" (with Melanie Tem)

(1) *Starshore* (mag., #2): McAlpine, Fall 1990.

(c) *In Concert* (with Melanie Tem) (collection of collaborations): Centipede Press, 2010.

"L Is For Love"

(1) *Footsteps* (mag., #8): Bill Munster, Nov. 1987.

"Labyrinthine"

(1) *Computer Gaming World* (mag., v.2, #5): Golden Empire Publications, Sept./Oct. 1982.

"La Mariee"

(1) *Art From Art* (anth., ed. Stephen Soucy): Modernist Press, 2011.

"Last Dragon"

(1) *Amazing Stories* (mag., v.62, #3): TSR, Inc., Sept. 1987.

(r) *A Dragon-Lover's Treasury of the Fantastic* (anth., ed. Margaret Weiss): Aspect/ Warner Books, 1994.

(c) *Celestial Inventories* (f.c.): ChiZine Publications, 2013.

"Last Drink Bird Head"

(1) *Last Drink Bird Head: Flash Fiction for Charity* (anth., ed. Ann Vandermeer and Jeff Vandermeer): The Ministry of Whimsy Press, 2009.

"The Last Moments Before Bed"

(1) *After Death...* (anth., ed. Eric J. Guignard): Dark Moon Books, 2013.

(c) *Out of the Dark: A Storybook of Horrors* (f.c.): Centipede Press, 2016.

(c) *Exploring Dark Short Fiction #1: A Primer to Steve Rasnic Tem* (f.c., ed. Eric J. Guignard): Dark Moon Books, 2017.

"Leaks"

(1) *Whispers VI* (anth., ed. Stuart Schiff): Doubleday, 1987.

(r) *The Best of Whispers* (anth., ed. Stuart Schiff): Borderlands Press, 1994.

(c) *The Far Side of the Lake* (f.c.): Ash-Tree Press, 2001.

"Lesser Fires" (with Melanie Tem)

(1) *Halloween: Magic, Mystery, and the Macabre* (anth., ed. Paula Guran): Prime Books, 2013.

"A Letter from the Emperor"

(1) *Asimov's Science Fiction* (mag., v.31, #1): Dell Magazines, Jan. 2010.

(r) *The Year's Best Science Fiction & Fantasy 2011* (anth., ed. Rich Horton): Prime Books, 2011.

(r) *Galactic Empires* (anth., ed. Neil Clarke): Night Shade Books, 2017.

(c) *Twember: Science Fiction Stories; Imaginings vol. 7* (f.c.): NewCon Press, 2013.

"A Letter Written to Gabriel After His Death"

(1) *Aspen Anthology 6* (anth., ed. J.D. Muller): Aspen Leaves, 1978.

"The Lie"

(1) *2 AM* (mag., #10): 2 AM Publications, Winter 1988.

"**L**ie Down with the Sun"

    (1) *Jimson Weed* (*unknown periodical*): *unknown publisher*, 1978.

"**L**ittle Cruelties"

    (1) *Cutting Edge* (anth., ed. Dennis Etchison): Doubleday, 1986.

    (c) *City Fishing* (f.c.): Silver Salamander Press, 2000.

"**T**he Little Dead Girl"

    (1) *Fantasy Macabre* (fanzine, #5): Richard H. Fawcett, 1985.

    (c) *The Far Side of the Lake* (f.c.): Ash-Tree Press, 2001.

"**L**ittle One"

    (1) *Unspoken Water* (journal, #1): Read Raw Press, 2013.

"**L**ittle Poucet"

    (1) *Snow White, Blood Red* (anth., ed. Ellen Datlow and Terri Windling): AvoNova/ William Morrow, 1993.

    (c) *Celestial Inventories* (f.c.): ChiZine Publications, 2013.

"**L**iving Arrangement"

    (1) *Crimewave 11: Ghosts* (anth., ed. Andy Cox): TTA Press, 2010.

    (c) *Ugly Behavior* (f.c.): New Pulp Press, 2012.

"**T**he Long Afternoon of the Human Race"

    (c) *Twember: Science Fiction Stories; Imaginings vol. 7* (f.c.): NewCon Press, 2013.

"**L**ong Fade Into Evening"

    (1) (forthcoming) *Darker Companions: Celebrating 50 Years of Ramsey Campbell* (anth., ed. Joseph Pulver and Scott Aniolowski): PS Publishing, 2017.

"**L**ong Haul"

    (1) *Mike Shayne Mystery Magazine* (mag., v.47, #3): Renown Publications, Inc., Mar. 1983.

"**L**ookie-loo"

    (1) *Turn Down the Lights (anth., ed.* Richard Chizmar): Chizmar Cemetery Dance Publications, 2013.

"Lost" (with Melanie Tem)
>   (1) *Imagination Fully Dilated* (anth., ed. Alan M. Clark and Elizabeth Engstrom): Cemetery Dance Publications, 1998.
>   (c) *In Concert* (with Melanie Tem) (collection of collaborations): Centipede Press, 2010.

"Lost Cherokee"
>   (1) *Tales from the Great Turtle* (anth., ed. Piers Anthony and Richard Gilliam): Tor, 1994.

"Lost in the Garden of Earthly Delights"
>   (1) *Shadow's Edge* (anth., ed. Simon Stranzas): Gray Friar Press, 2013.

"Mama" (with Melanie Tem)
>   (1) *Sisters of the Night* (anth., ed. Barbara Hambly and Martin H. Greenberg): Aspect/ Warner Books, 1995.
>   (c) *In Concert* (with Melanie Tem) (collection of collaborations): Centipede Press, 2010.

"The Man in the Rose Bushes"
>   (1) *Ghost and Scholars Book of Shadows: Volume* 3 (anth., ed. Rosemary Pardoe): Sarob Press, 2016.

"The Man on the Ceiling" (with Melanie Tem)
>   (1) (chapbook): American Fantasy, 2000.
>   (r) *The Year's Best Fantasy and Horror: Fourteenth Annual Collection* (anth., ed. Ellen Datlow and Terri Windling): St. Martin's Griffin, 2001.
>   (r) *Poe's Children: The New Horror* (anth., ed. Peter Straub): Doubleday Books 2008.
>   (c) *In Concert* (with Melanie Tem) (collection of collaborations): Centipede Press, 2010.

"The Man Under the Bridge"
>   (1) *Bruce Coville's Book of Spine Tinglers II: More Tales to Make You Shiver* (anth., ed. Bruce Coville): Apple/ Scholastic, 1997.

"The Man Who Made Plasticware"
> (1) *Gumbo* (*unknown periodical*): *unknown publisher*, 1978.

"Markers"
> (1) *Cemetery Dance* (mag., #2): Cemetery Dance Publications, June 1989.

"The Marriage" (with Melanie Tem)
> (1) *Love in Vein: Twenty Original Tales of Vampiric Erotica* (anth., ed. Poppy Z. Brite and Martin H. Greenberg): HarperPrism, 1994.
> (c) *In Concert* (with Melanie Tem) (collection of collaborations): Centipede Press, 2010.

"A Mask In My Sack"
> (1) *The Saint Magazine* (mag. (relaunch), v.1, #1): Halo Publications, Inc, June 1984.
> (c) *City Fishing* (f.c.): Silver Salamander Press, 2000.

"Mask of the Hero" (with Melanie Tem)
> (1) *Chilled To The Bone* (anth., ed. Robert Garcia): Mayfair Games, 1991.
> (c) *In Concert* (with Melanie Tem) (collection of collaborations): Centipede Press, 2010.

"The Masque of Edgar Allan Poe"
> (1) *Evermore* (anth., ed. James Robert Smith and Stephen Mark Rainey): Arkham House, 2006.
> (c) *Out of the Dark: A Storybook of Horrors* (f.c.): Centipede Press, 2016.

"Mechanic"
> (1) *Chrysalis 10* (anth., ed. Roy Torgeson): Doubleday, 1983.

"The Men and Women of Rivendale"
> (1) *Night Visions 1* (anth., ed. Alan Ryan): Dark Harvest, 1984.
> (r) *Vampires* (anth., ed. Alan Ryan): Doubleday, 1987.
> (r) *The Vampire Archives: The Most Complete Volume of Vampire*

Tales Ever Published (anth., ed. Otto Penzler): Vintage Crime/ Black Lizard/ Vintage Books, 2009.

(r) *Nightmare Magazine* (online media): nightmare-mag..com, Aug. 2015.

(c) *City Fishing* (f.c.): Silver Salamander Press, 2000.

"Merry-Go-Round"
(1) *New Pathways Into Science Fiction and Fantasy* (mag., #14): MGA Services, May 1989.
(c) *Onion Songs* (f.c.): Chomu Press, 2013.

"Merry X"
(1) (chapbook/ Christmas card): Wormhole Books, 2003.
(c) *Out of the Dark: A Storybook of Horrors* (f.c.): Centipede Press, 2016.

"The Messenger"
(1) *Weird Tales #3* (anth., ed. Lin Carter): Zebra Books/ Kensington Publishing Corp., Fall 1981.
(c) *Onion Songs* (f.c.): Chomu Press, 2013.

"Minimalist Biography"
(c) *Onion Songs* (f.c.): Chomu Press, 2013.

"Miranda Jo's Girl"
(1) *Appalachian Undead* (anth., ed. Eugene Johnson and Jason Sizemore): Apex Book Company, 2012.

"Miri"
(1) *Blood and Other Cravings* (anth., ed. Ellen Datlow): Tor, 2011.
(r) *The Mammoth Book of Best New Horror, Vol. 23* (anth., ed. Stephen Jones): Carroll & Graf/ Running Press, 2012.
(c) *Out of the Dark: A Storybook of Horrors* (f.c.): Centipede Press, 2016.

"Mirror Man"
(1) *Decoded Mirrors: 3 Tales After Lovecraft* (chapbook including 3 stories): Necronomicon Press, 1992.

    (r) *The Mammoth Book of Best New Horror, Vol. 4* (anth., ed. Stephen Jones and Ramsey Campbell): Carroll & Graf/ Running Press, 1993

    (r) *The Giant Book of Terror* (anth., ed. Stephen Jones and Ramsey Campbell): Magpie Books, 1994.

    (c) *The Far Side of the Lake* (f.c.): Ash-Tree Press, 2001.

"Mister Ainsley"

    (1) (forthcoming) *Black Wings VI: New Tales of Lovecraftian Horror* (anth., ed. S.T. Joshi): PS Publishing, 2017.

"Monkeys"

    (1) *The Mammoth Book of Jack the Ripper* (anth., ed. Maxim Jakubowski and Nathan Braund): Carroll & Graf, 2015.

"The Monster in the Field"

    (c) *Celestial Inventories* (f.c.): ChiZine Publications, 2013.

"The Monster Makers"

    (1) *Black Static* (mag., #35): TTA Press, Jul./Aug. 2013.

    (r) *The Best Horror of the Year Volume 6* (anth., ed. Ellen Datlow): Night Shade Books, 2014.

    (r) *The Monstrous* (anth., ed. Ellen Datlow): Tachyon Publications, 2015.

"More Than Should Be Asked" (with Melanie Tem)

    (1) *Scream Factory* (fanzine, #15): Deadline Press, Autumn 1994.

    (c) *In Concert* (with Melanie Tem) (collection of collaborations): Centipede Press, 2010.

"Morning Talk"

    (1) *Horrors* (anth., ed. Charles L. Grant): Playboy Paperbacks, 1981.

"Mother Hag"

    (1) *Grue Magazine* (mag., #5): Hell's Kitchen Productions, 1987.

    (r) *Tales By Moonlight II* (anth., ed. Jessica Salmonson): Tor, 1989.

    (c) *Out of the Dark: A Storybook of Horrors* (f.c.): Centipede Press, 2016.

"Motherson"
  (1) *Masques III* (anth., ed. J.N. Williamson): St. Martin's Press, 1989.
  (r) *Fleshcreepers: Startling New Works of Horror and the Supernatural* (anth., ed. J.N. Williamson): Robson Books, 1990.
  (r) *Darker Masques* (anth., ed. J.N. Williamson): Pinnacle Books/ Kensington Publishing Corp., 2002.

"The Moths"
  (1) *Weirdbook* (mag., #17): W. Paul Ganley, 1983.

"The Mouse's Bedtime Story"
  (1) *Bedtime Stories to Darken Your Dreams* (anth., ed. Bruce Holland Rogers): IFD Publishing, 1999.
  (c) *Celestial Inventories* (f.c.): ChiZine Publications, 2013.

"Mouths"
  (1) *100 Vicious Little Vampire Stories* (anth., ed. Stefan R. Dziemianowicz, Robert H. Weinberg, and Martin H. Greenberg): Barnes & Noble Books, 1995.
  (c) *City Fishing* (f.c.): Silver Salamander Press, 2000.

"Mr. Belano's Visit"
  (1) *Legends of the Mountain State 4* (anth., ed. Michael Knost): Woodland Press, 2010.

"The Multiples of Sorrow"
  (1) *Cinnibar's Gnosis (anth., ed.* Dan Ghetu): Ex Occidente, 2009.
  (c) *Onion Songs* (f.c.): Chomu Press, 2013.

"My Wife, with the Yellow Hair"
  (1) *2 AM* (mag., #15): 2 AM Publications, Spring 1990.

"Mysteries of the Colon"
  (1) *Corpse Blossoms* (anth., ed. Julia Sevin and R.J. Sevin): Creeping Hemlock Press, 2005.
  (c) *Out of the Dark: A Storybook of Horrors* (f.c.): Centipede Press, 2016.

"Night Cry"
>(1) *Eldritch Tales* (mag., #2): Yith Press, 1981.

"The Night Doctor"
>(1) *The Spectral Book of Horror Stories* (anth., ed. Mark Morris): Spectral Press, 2014.
>(r) *The Mammoth Book of Best New Horror, Vol. 26* (anth., ed. Stephen Jones): Carroll & Graf/ Running Press, 2015.

"Night, the Endless Snowfall" (Part 2 of *A Trilogy for Sleep*)
>(1) *Eldritch Tales* (mag., #12): Yith Press, 1986.
>(c) *Onion Songs* (f.c.): Chomu Press, 2013.

"The Night Market" (with Melanie Tem)
>(1) *Expiration Date* (anth., ed. Nancy Kilpatrick): Hades Publications, 2015.

"Noppero-Bo"
>(1) *Black Static* (mag., #8): TTA Press, Dec. 2008.
>(c) *Out of the Dark: A Storybook of Horrors* (f.c.): Centipede Press, 2016.

"No Rest for Those Who Can't Sleep"
>(1) *This Is Horror* (online media): thisishorror.co.uk, 2012.
>(c) *Out of the Dark: A Storybook of Horrors* (f.c.): Centipede Press, 2016.

"North" (with Melanie Tem)
>(1) *Extremes 2: Fantasy and Horror from the Ends of the Earth* (anth., ed. Brian A. Hopkins): Lone Wolf Publications, 2001.
>(c) *In Concert* (with Melanie Tem) (collection of collaborations): Centipede Press, 2010.

"Nvumbi" (with Melanie Tem)
>(1) *Xanadu* 3 (anth., ed. Jane Yolen): Tor, 1995.
>(c) *In Concert* (with Melanie Tem) (collection of collaborations): Centipede Press, 2010.

"Off the Map"
(1) *Albedo One* (mag., #35): Albedo One Productions, 2009.
(c) *Onion Songs* (f.c.): Chomu Press, 2013.

"The Old Man Beset by Demons"
(1) *Exotic Gothic 4 (Postscripts 28/29)* (anth., ed. Danel Olson): PS Publishing, 2012.
(c) *Out of the Dark: A Storybook of Horrors* (f.c.): Centipede Press, 2016.

"Old Men On Porches"
(1) *Specters in Coal Dust* (anth., ed. Michael Knost): Woodland Press, 2010.

"On a Path of Marigolds"
(1) *Fantasy Book* (fanzine, #6): Fantasy Book Enterprises, Nov. 1982.
(c) *Out of the Dark: A Storybook of Horrors* (f.c.): Centipede Press, 2016.

"Onion Song"
(c) *Onion Songs* (f.c.): Chomu Press, 2013.

"The Orchard"
(1) *Isaac Asimov's Science Fiction Magazine* (mag., v.7, #8): Davis Publications, Aug. 1983.

"Origami Bird"
(1) (chapbook/ Independence Day postcard): Wormhole Books, 2002.
(c) *Celestial Inventories* (f.c.): ChiZine Publications, 2013.

"Out Late in the Park"
(1) *Gathering the Bones: Thirty-Four Original Stories from the World's Masters of Horror* (anth., ed. Ramsey Campbell, Jack Dann, Dennis Etchison): Tor, 2003.
(c) *Onion Songs* (f.c.): Chomu Press, 2013.

"Out of Colorado"
>   (1) *High Fantastic: Colorado's Fantasy and Dark Fantasy* (anth., ed.
>   Steve Tem): Ocean View Books, 1995.

"Outside"
>   (1) *The Children of Cthulhu* (anth., ed. John Pelan and Benjamin
>   Adams): Del Rey, 2002.
>   (c) *Out of the Dark: A Storybook of Horrors* (f.c.): Centipede Press,
>   2016.

"The Overcoat"
>   (1) *Night Visions 1* (anth., ed. Alan Ryan): Dark Harvest Books,
>   1984.
>   (r) *100 Fiendish Little Frightmares* (anth., ed. Stefan R.
>   Dziemianowicz, Robert H. Weinberg, and Martin H.
>   Greenberg): Barnes & Noble Books, 1997.
>   (c) *City Fishing* (f.c.): Silver Salamander Press, 2000.

"The Owl With Human Eyes"
>   (1) *Quarry* (SF issue) (mag., v.30, #3): Quarry Press Inc., Summer
>   1981.

"The Painters Are Coming Today"
>   (1) *Other Worlds 1* (anth., ed. Roy Torgeson): Zebra Books/
>   Kensington Publishing Corp, 1979.
>   (r) *100 Great Fantasy Short Shorts*, (anth., ed. Martin H. Greenberg,
>   Terry Carr, and Isaac Asimov): Doubleday, 1984.
>   (c) *City Fishing* (f.c.): Silver Salamander Press, 2000.

"Pareidolia"
>   (c) *City Fishing* (f.c.): Silver Salamander Press, 2000.
>   (r) *The Mammoth Book of Best New Horror, Vol. 12* (anth., ed.
>   Stephen Jones): Carroll & Graf/ Running Press, 2001.

"The Passing"
>   (1) *Mountain Magic* (anth., ed. Brian J. Hatcher): Woodland Press,
>   2010.

"Passing Through"

(1) *Deathport* (anth., ed. Ramsey Campbell): Pocket Books, 1993.

(c) *Out of the Dark: A Storybook of Horrors* (f.c.): Centipede Press, 2016.

"Pastel"

(c) *Out of the Dark: A Storybook of Horrors* (f.c.): Centipede Press, 2016.

"Pathetic Fallacy"

(1) *Tomorrow Speculative Fiction* (mag., #5): The Unifont Company, Inc., Oct. 1993.

(c) *Twember: Science Fiction Stories; Imaginings vol. 7* (f.c.): NewCon Press, 2013.

"Paula Breaks"

(1) *Surreal Worlds* (anth., ed. Sean Leonard: Bizarro Pulp Press/JournalStone, 2015.

"The Perfect Diamond" (with Melanie Tem)

(1) *Fantastic Worlds* (fanzine, v.1, #1): Scott A. Becker, 1996.

(c) *In Concert* (with Melanie Tem) (collection of collaborations): Centipede Press, 2010.

"Photograph"

(c) *Out of the Dark: A Storybook of Horrors* (f.c.): Centipede Press, 2016.

(r) *The Year's Best Dark Fantasy & Horror 2017 Edition* (anth., ed. Paula Guran): Prime Books, 2017.

"Piano Moon"

(1) *The Horror Show* (mag., v.3, #1): Phantasm Press, Winter 1985.

(r) *Best of the Horror Show: An Adventure in Terror* (anth., ed. David B. Silva): 2 AM Publications, 1987.

(r) *Definitive Best of The Horror Show (anth., ed. David B. Silva):* Cemetery Dance Publications, 1992.

"Picnic"

(c) *Onion Songs* (f.c.): Chomu Press, 2013.

"**P**illows"

    (1) *Portents* (anth., ed. Al Sarrantonio): Flying Fox Publishers, 2011.

    (c) *Out of the Dark: A Storybook of Horrors* (f.c.): Centipede Press, 2016.

"**P**it's Edge" (with Melanie Tem)

    (1) *Mondo Zombie* (anth., ed. John Skipp): Cemetery Dance Publications, 2006.

    (c) *In Concert* (with Melanie Tem) (collection of collaborations): Centipede Press, 2010.

"**P**lainclothes"

    (1) *Cemetery Dance* (mag., #10): Cemetery Dance Publications, Fall 1991.

    (r) *The Best of Cemetery Dance* (anth., ed. Richard Chizmar): Cemetery Dance Publications, 1998.

"**P**laying Dead"

    (1) *Marion Zimmer Bradley's Fantasy Magazine* (mag., #10): Marion Zimmer Bradley Ltd., Autumn 1990.

    (c) *Out of the Dark: A Storybook of Horrors* (f.c.): Centipede Press, 2016.

"The **P**oor"

    (1) *Terrors* (anth., ed. Charles L. Grant): Playboy Paperbacks, 1982.

    (r) *100 Great Fantasy Short Short Stories* (anth., ed. by Isaac Asimov, Terry Carr, and Martin H. Greenberg): Avon, 1984.

    (r) *100 Hair-raising Little Horror Stories* (anth., ed. Al Sarrantonio and Martin H. Greenberg): Barnes & Noble Books, 1993.

    (c) *City Fishing* (f.c.): Silver Salamander Press, 2000.

"**P**reparations for the Game"

    (1) *Whispers* (digest, #17/18): Stuart David Schiff, Aug. 1982.

    (r) *Masters of Darkness* (anth., ed. Dennis Etchison): Tor, 1980.

    (r) *100 Tiny Tales of Terror* (anth., ed. Stefan R. Dziemianowicz, Robert H. Weinberg, and Martin H. Greenberg): Barnes & Noble Books, 1996.

(c) *City Fishing* (f.c.): Silver Salamander Press, 2000.

"Presage"

(1) *All Hallows* (mag., #8): The Ghost Story Society, Feb. 1995.

(c) *The Far Side of the Lake* (f.c.): Ash-Tree Press, 2001.

"The Process"

(1) *Gauntlet* (mag., #3): Barry Hoffman, 1992.

"Prosthesis" (with Melanie Tem)

(1) *Isaac Asimov's Science Fiction Magazine* (mag., v.10, #6): Davis Publications, June 1986.

(c) *In Concert* (with Melanie Tem) (collection of collaborations): Centipede Press, 2010.

"Pulled Down to Sleep" (Part 1 of *A Trilogy for Sleep*)

(1) *Eldritch Tales* (mag., #11): Yith Press, 1985.

(c) *Out of the Dark: A Storybook of Horrors* (f.c.): Centipede Press, 2016.

"Punishment"

(1) *Night Visions 1* (anth., ed. Alan Ryan): Dark Harvest, 1984.

"The Rains"

(1) *Dark Terrors 2* (anth., ed. Stephen Jones and David Sutton): Gollancz, 1996.

(c) *City Fishing* (f.c.): Silver Salamander Press, 2000.

"Rat Catcher"

(1) *Dark at Heart* (anth., ed. Joe R. Lansdale and Karen Lansdale): Dark Harvest Books, 1992.

(r) *The Year's Best Fantasy and Horror: Sixth Annual Collection* (anth., ed. Ellen Datlow and Terri Windling): St. Martin's Griffin, 1993.

(c) *Ugly Behavior* (f.c.): New Pulp Press, 2012.

(c) *Exploring Dark Short Fiction #1: A Primer to Steve Rasnic Tem* (f.c., ed. Eric J. Guignard): Dark Moon Books, 2017.

"Re: Vision"

    (1) *Swashbuckling Editor Stories* (anth., ed. John Gregory Betancourt): Borgo Press, 1993.

    (r) *Pulphouse: A Fiction Magazine* (mag., #12/13): Pulphouse Publishing, Sept./Oct. 1992.

"Red Light"

    (1) *The Bleeding Edge* (anth., ed. William Nolan and Jason V Brock): Cycatrix Press, 2009.

    (c) *Out of the Dark: A Storybook of Horrors* (f.c.): Centipede Press, 2016.

"Red Rabbit"

    (1) *Borderlands 6* (anth., ed. Olivia F. Monteleone and Thomas F. Monteleone): Samhain Publishing, 2016.

    (r) *The Best Horror of the Year Volume 9* (anth., ed. Ellen Datlow): Night Shade Books, 2017.

"The Regulars"

    (1) *After Hours* (mag., #10): William G. Raley, Spring 1991.

    (c) *Out of the Dark: A Storybook of Horrors* (f.c.): Centipede Press, 2016.

"The Reincarnation"

    (1) *Pig Iron: Science Fiction* (anth., #10 in a series, ed. Rose Sayre and Jim Villani): Pig Iron Press, 1982.

"Release of Flesh"

    (1) *Hot Blood 4: Deadly After Dark* (anth., ed. Jeff Gelb and Michael Garrett): Pocket Books, 1994.

"Resettling" (with Melanie Tem)

    (1) *Post Mortem: New Tales of Ghostly Horror* (anth., ed. David B. Silva and Paul F. Olson): St. Martin's Press, 1989.

    (c) *In Concert* (with Melanie Tem) (collection of collaborations): Centipede Press, 2010.

"Rider"

    (1) *Night Visions 1* (anth., ed. Alan Ryan): Dark Harvest, 1984.

(c) *The Far Side of the Lake* (f.c.): Ash-Tree Press, 2001.

"The Rifleman, the Cancerous Cow, and the Swedish Memorial Hospital"
>   (1) *Pig Iron: Science Fiction* (anth., #11 in a series, ed. Rose Sayre and Jim Villani): Pig Iron Press, 1983.
>   (c) *Onion Songs* (f.c.): Chomu Press, 2013.

"Riverbanks"
>   (1) *Grue Magazine* (mag., #9): Hell's Kitchen Productions, 1989.

"Robin in the Mists"
>   (1) *The Fantastic Adventures of Robin Hood* (anth., ed. Martin H. Greenberg): Signet/ New American Library, 1991.

"The Sadness"
>   (1) *Star*Line* (mag., v.32, #6): SFPA, Nov./ Dec. 2009.
>   (c) *Onion Songs* (f.c.): Chomu Press, 2013.

"The Sadness of Angels"
>   (c) *City Fishing* (f.c.): Silver Salamander Press, 2000.

"Safe At Home" (with Melanie Tem)
>   (1) *Hottest Blood* 3: *The Ultimate in Erotic Horror* (anth., ed. Jeff Gelb and Michael Garrett): Pocket Books, 1993.
>   (r) *The Mammoth Book of Best New Horror, Vol. 5* (anth., ed. Stephen Jones and Ramsey Campbell): Carroll & Graf, 1994.
>   (c) *In Concert* (with Melanie Tem) (collection of collaborations): Centipede Press, 2010.

"Safe House"
>   (1) *Winter Chills* (mag., #3): The British Fantasy Society, 1989.
>   (c) *City Fishing* (f.c.): Silver Salamander Press, 2000.

"Saguaro Night"
>   (c) *Ugly Behavior* (f.c.): New Pulp Press, 2012.
>   (r) *Great Jones Street* (online app): greatjonesstreet.press, 2017.

"Saleb"
(1) *Juice* (mag., #5): *unknown publisher,* 1977.

"Sampled"
(1) *Dark Terrors: The Gollancz Book of Horror* (anth., ed. Stephen Jones and David Sutton): Gollancz, 1995.

"Saturday"
(c) *Onion Songs* (f.c.): Chomu Press, 2013.

"Saturday Afternoon"
(1) *Brutarian* (mag., #33): Odium Enterprises, Spring 2001.
(c) *Onion Songs* (f.c.): Chomu Press, 2013.

"Save the Children!"
(1) *Weird Tales #4* (anth., ed. Lin Carter): Zebra Books/ Kensington Publishing Corp., Summer 1983.
(r) *Weird Tales: Seven Decades of Terror* (anth., ed. John Betancourt and Robert Weinberg): Barnes & Noble Books, 1997.

"Scree"
(1) *Cemetery Dance* (mag., #66): Cemetery Dance Publications, 2012.
(c) *Out of the Dark: A Storybook of Horrors* (f.c.): Centipede Press, 2016.

"S.D. Watkins Painter of Portraits"
(1) *Visitants: Stories of Fallen Angels & Heavenly Hosts* (anth., ed. Stephen Jones): Ulysses Press, 2010.
(c) *Out of the Dark: A Storybook of Horrors* (f.c.): Centipede Press, 2016.

"The Secret Flesh"
(1) *Pulphouse: The Hardback Magazine* (mag., #11): Pulphouse Publishing, Spring 1991.
(c) *Celestial Inventories* (f.c.): ChiZine Publications, 2013.

"The Secret Laws of the Universe"
(1) *Psycho-Mania!* (anth., ed. Stephen Jones): Robinson, 2013.

"Seeing the Trees"
(1) *Matter* (*unknown periodical, #*11): *unknown publisher*, 2008.
(c) *Here With the Shadows* (f.c.): Swan River Press, 2014.

"Self-Possessed"
(1) *The Horror Show* (mag., v.4, #4): Phantasm Press, Fall 1986.
(r) *Definitive Best of The Horror Show (anth., ed.* David B. Silva): Cemetery Dance Publications, 1992.
(c) *Out of the Dark: A Storybook of Horrors* (f.c.): Centipede Press, 2016.

"Shades" (with Roma Felible)
(1) *Flesh Fantastic* (anth., ed. Amarantha Knight): Masquerade Books/ Rhinoceros Publications, 1994.

"Shadow"
(1) *Poe: 19 New Tales of Suspense, Dark Fantasy and Horror* (anth., ed. Ellen Datlow): Solaris, 2009.
(c) *Out of the Dark: A Storybook of Horrors* (f.c.): Centipede Press, 2016.

"Shadows in the Grass"
(1) *The 19th Fontana Book of Great Horror Stories* (anth., ed. R. Chetwynd Hayes): Fontana, 1983.
(r) *100 Ghastly Little Ghost Stories* (anth., ed. Stefan R. Dziemianowicz, Robert H. Weinberg, and Martin H. Greenberg): Barnes & Noble Books, 1993.
(r) *Tales to Freeze the Blood* (anth., ed. R. Chetwynd Hayes and Stephen Jones): Running Press, 2006.
(c) *Out of the Dark: A Storybook of Horrors* (f.c.): Centipede Press, 2016.

"Shaggy Dog Story"
(1) *Blood Lite II: Overbite* (anth., ed. Kevin Anderson): Gallery Books, 2010.
(c) *Out of the Dark: A Storybook of Horrors* (f.c.): Centipede Press, 2016.

"Sharp Edges"

> (1) *Dark Terrors 3: The Gollancz Book of Horror* (anth., ed. Stephen Jones and David Sutton): Gollancz, 1997.
>
> (c) *Ugly Behavior* (f.c.): New Pulp Press, 2012.

"Shoplifter"

> (1) *Kayak* (mag., #60): *unknown publisher*, 1982.
>
> (c) *Onion Songs* (f.c.): Chomu Press, 2013.

"Show Night"

> (1) *Dark Discoveries* (mag., #13): Dark Discoveries Publications, Spring 2009.
>
> (r) *Discoveries Best of Horror & Dark Fantasy* (anth., ed. James Beach and Jason V Brock): Dark Discoveries Publications, 2015.
>
> (r) *The Mammoth Book of Kaiju* (anth., ed. Sean Wallace): Prime Books, 2016.

"Shuffle"

> (c) *Onion Songs* (f.c.): Chomu Press, 2013.

"The Sing" (with Melanie Tem)

> (1) *SF International* (mag., #1): Andromeda Press, Jan./Feb. 1987.
>
> (c) *In Concert* (with Melanie Tem) (collection of collaborations): Centipede Press, 2010.

"Sirens"

> (1) *Weird Tales* (mag., v.53, #4 (305)): Terminus, Winter 1992/1993.

"Skullbees"

> (1) Included in the Centipede Press edition of the novel, *Deadfall Hotel*, 2012.

"The Sky Came Down to Earth"

> (1) *Tales by Moonlight* (anth., ed. Jessica Salmonson): Robert T. Garcia, 1983.
>
> (c) *The Far Side of the Lake* (f.c.): Ash-Tree Press, 2001.

"Slapstick"

(1) *Bare Bone #11* (anth., ed. Kevin L. Donihe): Raw Dog Screaming Press, 2009.

(c) *Onion Songs* (f.c.): Chomu Press, 2013.

"Sleep"

(1) *Rod Serling's The Twilight Zone Magazine* (mag., issue v1 #12): TZ Publications, Mar. 1982.

(r) *100 Great Fantasy Short Short Stories* (anth., ed. by Isaac Asimov, Terry Carr, and Martin H. Greenberg): Avon, 1984.

(c) *Out of the Dark: A Storybook of Horrors* (f.c.): Centipede Press, 2016.

"Sleeping Ute"

(1) *Dark Discoveries* (mag., #23): JournalStone, Spring 2013.

(c) *Out of the Dark: A Storybook of Horrors* (f.c.): Centipede Press, 2016.

"Sleepless"

(1) (forthcoming) *Crimewave 13* (anth., ed. Andy Cox): TTA Press, 2017.

"The Slow Fall of Dust in a Quiet Place"

(1) *Shadows and Silence* (anth., ed. Barbara Roden and Christopher Roden): Ash-Tree Press, 2000.

(c) *Here With the Shadows* (f.c.): Swan River Press, 2014.

"A Small Room"

(1) (chapbook): Biting Dog (Shocklines), 2005

(c) *Out of the Dark: A Storybook of Horrors* (f.c.): Centipede Press, 2016.

"Smoke in a Bottle"

(1) *Appalachian Winter Hauntings* (anth., ed. Michael Knost and Mark Justice) Woodland Press, 2009.

(r) *All-American Horror of the 21ˢᵗ Century* (anth., ed. Mort Castle): Independent Legions Publishing, 2013.

(c) *Here With the Shadows* (f.c.): Swan River Press, 2014.

"The Snow People"
> (1) *Fantasy Macabre* (fanzine, #14): Richard H. Fawcett, 1992.
> (c) *The Far Side of the Lake* (f.c.): Ash-Tree Press, 2001.

"Sometimes I Get Lost"
> (1) *Electric Velocipede* (mag., #11): Spilt Milk Press, Fall 2006.
> (c) *Onion Songs* (f.c.): Chomu Press, 2013.

"The Soul As Mickey Mouse"
> (1) *Jimson Weed* (*unknown periodical*): *unknown publisher*, 1978.

"The Sound of Hawkwings Dissolving"
> (1) *Chrysalis* 9 (anth., ed. Roy Torgeson): Doubleday, 1981.

"Spidertalk"
> (1) *Night Visions* 1 (anth., ed. Alan Ryan): Dark Harvest, 1984.
> (r) *100 Creepy Little Creature Stories* (anth., ed. Stefan R. Dziemianowicz, Robert H. Weinberg, and Martin H. Greenberg): Barnes & Noble Books, 1994.
> (c) *Out of the Dark: A Storybook of Horrors* (f.c.): Centipede Press, 2016.

"Spirited"
> (1) *Taverns of the Dead* (anth., ed. Patrick Kealan Burke): Cemetery Dance Publications, 2005.
> (c) *Out of the Dark: A Storybook of Horrors* (f.c.): Centipede Press, 2016.

"Squeezer"
> (1) *New Crimes No. 3* (anth., ed. Maxim Jakubowski): Carroll & Graf, 1991.
> (c) *Ugly Behavior* (f.c.): New Pulp Press, 2012.

"The Stench"
> (1) *Shivers V* (anth., ed. Richard Chizmar): Cemetery Dance Publications, 2008.
> (c) *Ugly Behavior* (f.c.): New Pulp Press, 2012.

"Stick Men"

(1) *Jamais Vu* (journal, issue 3): Post Mortem Press, Autumn 2014.

"Still, Cold Air"

(c) *Here With the Shadows* (f.c.): Swan River Press, 2014.

(r) *The Year's Best Dark Fantasy & Horror 2015 Edition* (anth., ed. Paula Guran): Prime Books, 2015.

"Stone Head"

(1) *Shadows* 5 (anth., ed. Charles L. Grant): Doubleday, 1982.

(c) *The Far Side of the Lake* (f.c.): Ash-Tree Press, 2001.

"Stones"

(1) *New Crimes No. 2* (anth., ed. Maxim Jakubowski): Constable and Robinson, 1990.

(c) *Ugly Behavior* (f.c.): New Pulp Press, 2012.

"Strands"

(1) *Nøctulpa* (journal, #4): Horror's Head Press, Spring 1990.

(c) *Onion Songs* (f.c.): Chomu Press, 2013.

"Strangeness"

(1) *Sybil's Garage* (mag., #4): Senses Five Press, 2007.

(c) *Onion Songs* (f.c.): Chomu Press, 2013.

"The Strangers"

(1) *Scare Care* (anth., ed. Graham Masterton): Tor, 1989.

(c) *Out of the Dark: A Storybook of Horrors* (f.c.): Centipede Press, 2016.

"Taking Down the Tree"

(1) *Pulphouse: A Fiction Magazine* (mag., #8): Pulphouse Publishing, Dec. 1991.

(r) *The Mammoth Book of Best New Horror, Vol. 3* (anth., ed. Stephen Jones and Ramsey Campbell): Carroll & Graf, 1992.

(c) *City Fishing* (f.c.): Silver Salamander Press, 2000.

"Teddy Bear Winter"

(1) *Magic Realism* (mag., #4): Pyx Press, Fall 1991.

"Telling"
- (1) *The Seventh Black Book of Horror* (anth., ed. Charles Black): Mortbury Press, 2010.
- (r) *The Mammoth Book of Best New Horror, Vol. 22* (anth., ed. Stephen Jones): Carroll & Graf/ Running Press, 2011.
- (c) *Here With the Shadows* (f.c.): Swan River Press, 2014.

"Ten Things I Know About the Wizard"
- (1) *Fantasy Book* (fanzine, v.2, #2): Fantasy Book Enterprises, May 1983.
- (r) *The Mammoth Book of Sorcerers' Tales* (anth., ed. Mike Ashley): Carroll & Graf/ Robinson, 2004; retitled *Mammoth Book of Black Magic* (anth., ed. Mike Ashley): Running Press/ Robinson, 2012.

"The Tenth Scholar" (with Melanie Tem)
- (1) *The Ultimate Dracula* (anth., ed. Megan Miller, David Keller, and Byron Preiss): Dell, 1991.
- (r) *The Year's Best Fantasy and Horror: Fifth Annual Collection* (anth., ed. Ellen Datlow and Terri Windling): St. Martin's Griffin, 1992.
- (c) *In Concert* (with Melanie Tem) (collection of collaborations): Centipede Press, 2010.

"There's No Such Thing as Monsters"
- (1) *Fantasy & Terror* (mag., #3): Richard Fawcett, 1984.
- (r) *100 Creepy Little Creature Stories* (anth., ed. Stefan R. Dziemianowicz, Robert H. Weinberg, and Martin H. Greenberg): Barnes & Noble Books, 1994.
- (r) *Bedtime Stories to Darken Your Dreams* (anth., ed. Bruce Holland Rogers): IFD Publishing, 1999.

"These Days When All is Silver and Bright"
- (1) *Supernatural Tales* (periodical, #21): David Longhorn, Summer 2012.
- (c) *Here With the Shadows* (f.c.): Swan River Press, 2014.

"A Thin Silver Line"
(1) scheduled for *The Last Dangerous Visions* (anth., ed. Harlan Ellison).

"This Icy Region My Heart Encircles" (with Melanie Tem)
(1) *The Ultimate Frankenstein* (anth., ed. Megan Miller, David Keller, Byron Preiss, and John Betancourt): Dell, 1991.
(c) *In Concert* (with Melanie Tem) (collection of collaborations): Centipede Press, 2010.

"This Thing Called Love"
(1) *Tourniquet Heart* (anth., ed. Christopher Teague): Prime Books, 2002.

"The Three Billy Goats Gruff"
(1) *Grue Magazine* (mag., #3): Hell's Kitchen Productions, 1986.
(c) *Out of the Dark: A Storybook of Horrors* (f.c.): Centipede Press, 2016.

"Thrumm"
(1) *In Dreams* (anth., ed. Paul J. McAuley and Kim Newman): Gollancz, 1992.
(c) *City Fishing* (f.c.): Silver Salamander Press, 2000.

"Time and the Exile"
(1) *ConAdian Souvenir Book*, (anth., ed. Shannon Reschke): ConAdian, 1994.

"To Denver (with Hiram battling zombies)"
(1) *Zombies VS Robots: This is War* (anth., ed. Jeff Conner): IDW Publishing, 2012.

"Too Many Ghosts"
(1) *The Dark* (e-mag., #19): Prime Books, Dec. 2016.

"Torn"
(1) *I Am the Abyss* (anth., ed. Chris Morey): Dark Regions Press, 2017.

"Tricks & Treats: One Night on Halloween Street"
    (1) *The Magazine of Fantasy & Science Fiction* (digest, v.97, #6): Mercury Press, Dec. 1999.
    (r) *The Mammoth Book of Best New Horror, Vol. 11* (anth., ed. Stephen Jones): Carroll & Graf/ Running Press, 2000.
    (r) *Halloween* (anth., ed. Paula Guran): Prime Books, 2011.
    (c) *Out of the Dark: A Storybook of Horrors* (f.c.): Centipede Press, 2016.

"Trickster"
    (1) *Halloween Horrors*, (anth., ed. Alan Ryan): Doubleday, 1986.
    (c) *City Fishing* (f.c.): Silver Salamander Press, 2000.

"A Trip into the Country"
    (1) *White Cat Magazine* (online media): whitecatpublications.com, Jan. 2012.
    (c) *Out of the Dark: A Storybook of Horrors* (f.c.): Centipede Press, 2016.

"Twember"
    (1) *Interzone* (mag., #239): TTA Press, Mar./Apr. 2012.
    (r) *Mammoth Book of Time Travel SF* (anth., ed. Mike Ashley): Robinson, 2013.
    (r) *Time Travel: Recent Trips* (anth., ed. Paula Guran): Prime Books, 2014.
    (c) *Twember: Science Fiction Stories; Imaginings vol. 7* (f.c.): NewCon Press, 2013.

"Tyger"
    (1) *Night Terrors III* (anth., ed. G. Winston Hyatt, Marc Ciccarone, and Theresa Dillon): Blood Bound Books, 2014.

"Ugly Behavior"
    (1) *Out of the Gutter* (mag., #7): Gutter Books, Winter 2010.
    (c) *Ugly Behavior* (f.c.): New Pulp Press, 2012.

"Umbrellas"
    (1) *Nocturne* (mag., #1): Michael J. Lotus and Vincent L. Michael,

Autumn 1988.

"Underground"

(1) *Metahorror* (anth., ed. Dennis Etchison): Abyss/ Dell, 1992.

(c) *The Far Side of the Lake* (f.c.): Ash-Tree Press, 2001.

"Unknown"

(1) *Black Static* (mag., #2): TTA Press, Dec. 2007.

(c) *Onion Songs* (f.c.): Chomu Press, 2013.

"The Unmasking"

(1) *Phantoms* (anth., ed. Martin H. Greenberg): DAW Books, 1989.

(r) *Tales From the Crossroad Volume One* (anth., ed. David Niall Wilson and David Dodd): Crossroad Press, 2011.

(c) *Out of the Dark: A Storybook of Horrors* (f.c.): Centipede Press, 2016.

"Vintage Domestic"

(1) *The Mammoth Book of Vampire Stories* (anth., ed. Stephen Jones): Carroll & Graf, 1992.

(r) *100 Vicious Little Vampire Stories* (anth., ed. Stefan R. Dziemianowicz, Robert H. Weinberg, and Martin H. Greenberg): Barnes & Noble Books, 1995.

(c) *Out of the Dark: A Storybook of Horrors* (f.c.): Centipede Press, 2016.

"The Visible Man"

(1) *New Pathways* (mag., #17): MGA Services, Sept. 1990.

(c) *City Fishing* (f.c.): Silver Salamander Press, 2000.

"A Visit Home"

(1) *The Tiger Garden* (anth., ed. Nicholas Royle): Serpent's Tail, 1996.

(c) *Onion Songs* (f.c.): Chomu Press, 2013.

"Visitors"

(1) *Asimov's Science Fiction* (mag., v.35, #1): Dell Magazines, Jan. 2011.

(c) *Twember: Science Fiction Stories; Imaginings vol. 7* (f.c.): NewCon Press, 2013.

"Voices in the Dark"
(1) *Horrors! 365 Scary Stories* (anth., ed. Stefan R. Dziemianowicz, Robert H. Weinberg, and Martin H. Greenberg): Barnes & Noble Books, 1998.

"Vulture"
(1) *The Further Adventures of Batman, Vol. 2, Featuring the Penguin* (anth., ed. Martin H. Greenberg): Spectra, 1992.

"Waiting At The Crossroads Motel"
(1) *Black Wings II: New Tales of Lovecraftian Horror* (anth., ed. S.T. Joshi): PS Publishing, 2012.
(r) *The Mammoth Book of Best New Horror, Vol. 24* (anth., ed. Stephen Jones): Robinson/ Running Press, 2013.
(r) *Lovecraft's Monsters* (anth., ed. Ellen Datlow): Tachyon Publications, 2014.
(c) *Out of the Dark: A Storybook of Horrors* (f.c.): Centipede Press, 2016.

"Wake" (Part 3 of *A Trilogy for Sleep*)
(1) *Eldritch Tales* (mag., #13): Yith Press, 1985.

"The Wake"
(1) *Nightmare's Realm: New Tales of the Weird & Fantastic* (anth., ed. S.T. Joshi): Dark Regions Press, 2017

"Wanderlust"
(1) *Tales of the Wandering Jew* (anth., ed. Brian Stableford): Daedalus, 1991.

"War on the Downside"
(1) *Extro Science Fiction* (mag., #3): Specifi Publications, July/Aug. 1982.

"We All Live On Sycamore Street"
(1) *World Horror 2000 Convention Book* (anth.): Horror Writers

Association, 2000.

(c) Out of the Dark: A Storybook of Horrors (f.c.): Centipede Press, 2016.

"The Weight Lost"

(1) *A Darke Phantastique* (anth., ed. Jason V Brock): Cycatrix Press, 2015.

"Welcome to Rodeomart"

(1) *Subtle Edens* (anth., ed. Allen Ashley): Elastic Press, 2008.

"Wet Kisses in the Dark"

(1) *Hardboiled* (mag., #23) *unknown publisher*, 1997.

(c) *Ugly Behavior* (f.c.): New Pulp Press, 2012.

(r) *Great Jones Street* (online app): greatjonesstreet.press, 2017.

"What Slips Away"

(1) *More Monsters from Memphis* (anth., ed. Beecher Smith): Zapizdat Publications, 1998.

(r) *The Mammoth Book of Best New Horror, Vol. 10* (anth., ed. Stephen Jones): Carroll & Graf/ Robinson, 1999.

(c) *Out of the Dark: A Storybook of Horrors* (f.c.): Centipede Press, 2016.

"Whatever You Want"

(c) *Exploring Dark Short Fiction #1: A Primer to Steve Rasnic Tem* (f.c., ed. Eric J. Guignard): Dark Moon Books, 2017.

"Wheatfield with Crows"

(1) *Dark World: Ghost Stories* (anth., ed. Timothy Parker Russell): Tartarus Press, 2013.

(r) *The Year's Best Dark Fantasy & Horror 2014 Edition* (anth., ed. Paula Guran): Prime Books, 2014.

(r) *The Dark* (e-mag., #15): Prime Books, Aug. 2016.

(c) *Here With the Shadows* (f.c.): Swan River Press, 2014.

"When Coyote Takes Back the World"

(1) Lands of Never: Anthology of Modern Fantasy (anth., ed.

Maxim Jakubowski): Allen & Unwin, 1983.
(c) *City Fishing* (f.c.): Silver Salamander Press, 2000.

"When We Moved On"
  (1) *Clockwork Phoenix 2* (anth., ed. Mike Allen): Norilana Books, 2009.
  (c) *Celestial Inventories* (f.c.): ChiZine Publications, 2013.

"White Rose"
  (1) *Quarry* (SF issue) (mag., v.30, #3): Quarry Press Inc., Summer 1981.

"Willie the Philologist"
  (1) *Now & Then: The Appalachian Magazine* (mag., v.26, #2): East Tennessee State University, 2010.
  (r) *30 Years, Best of Now & Then, Part II (2000–2014)* (mag., v.31, #1): East Tennessee State University, Summer 2015.

"Woman On The Corner"
  (1) *Whispers* (digest, #23/24): Stuart David Schiff, Oct. 1987.
  (c) *City Fishing* (f.c.): Silver Salamander Press, 2000.

"The Woodcarver's Son"
  (1) *Offworld* (mag., #2): Graphic Image Press, Winter 1993/94.
  (c) *Celestial Inventories* (f.c.): ChiZine Publications, 2013.

"The World Recalled"
  (1) (chapbook): Wormhole Books, 2005.
  (c) *Celestial Inventories* (f.c.): ChiZine Publications, 2013.

"The World through the Tree"
  (1) *Mythellany* (mag., #4): Mythopoeic Society, 1984.

"Worms"
  (1) *Night Visions 1* (anth., ed. Alan Ryan): Dark Harvest, 1984.
  (c) *Out of the Dark: A Storybook of Horrors* (f.c.): Centipede Press, 2016.

"Writing in the Dark"

(1) *After Hours* (mag., #11): William G. Raley, Summer 1991.

"Yesterday"
> (1) *Quietly Now* (anth., ed. Kealan Patrick Burke): Borderlands Press, 2004.
>
> (c) *Out of the Dark: A Storybook of Horrors* (f.c.): Centipede Press, 2016.

"You Dreamed It"
> (1) *The Saint Magazine* (mag., #2): Halo Publications, Inc., July 1984.
>
> (c) *Ugly Behavior* (f.c.): New Pulp Press, 2012.

"Your Daughter is Here"
> (c) *Out of the Dark: A Storybook of Horrors* (f.c.): Centipede Press, 2016.

NOVELS, CHAPBOOKS, and OTHER SINGLE WORKS

12 Minutes of Darkness (chapbook) (dually published with chapbook, *Celestial Inventory*): Chris Drumm (Drumm Booklet), 1991 (contents also included in the collection *Onion Songs*).

Absences: Charlie Goode's Ghosts—Haunted Library "Psychic Sleuths' Booklet Number Two" (chapbook including 6 stories): Haunted Library, 1991. (contents also included in the collection *The Far Side of the Lake* and the ebook *Absent Company*).

Among the Living (novelette): Delirium Books, 2011 (contents also included in the ebook *Absent Company*).

Beautiful Strangers (with Melanie Tem) (chapbook): Roadkill Press, 1992 (contents also included in the collection *In Concert*).

Blood Kin (novel): Solaris, 2014.

The Book of Days (novel): Subterranean Press, 2003; (ebook): Crossroad Press/Macabre Ink, 2010.

Celestial Inventory (chapbook; Drumm Booklet #36) (dually published with chapbook, *12 Minutes of Darkness*): Chris Drumm (Drumm Booklet), 1991 (contents also included in the collection *Celestial Inventories*).

Daughters (with Melanie Tem) (novel): iPublish/TimeWarner, 2001; (ebook): Crossroad Press/Mystique Press, 2010.

Deadfall Hotel (novel): Solaris, 2012; (hardcover): Centipede Press, 2011.

Decoded Mirrors: 3 Tales After Lovecraft (chapbook including 3 stories): Necronomicon Press, 1992 (contents also included in the collections *The Far Side of the Lake* and *Out of the Dark: A Storybook of Horrors*).

Excavation (novel): Avon, 1987; (hardcover): Delirium Dark Essentials, 2006; (ebook): Crossroad Press/Macabre Ink, 2010.

Fairytales (chapbook): Roadkill Press, 1990 (contents also included in the collection *City Fishing*).

In the Lovecraft Museum (novella): PS Publishing, 2015.

In These Final Days of Sales (chapbook): Wormhole Books, 2001 (contents also included in the collection *Celestial Inventories*).

The Man on the Ceiling (with Melanie Tem) (chapbook): American Fantasy, 2000 (contents also included in the collection *In Concert*).

The Man on the Ceiling (with Melanie Tem) (novel): Wizards of the Coast Discoveries, 2008; (ebook): Crossroad Press, 2013.

A Small Room (chapbook): Biting Dog (Shocklines), 2005 (contents also included in the collection *Out of the Dark*).

UBO (novel): Solaris, 2017.

The World Recalled (chapbook): Wormhole Books, 2005 (contents also included in the collection *Celestial Inventories*).

Yours to Tell: Dialogues on the Art & Practice of Writing (with Melanie Tem) (nonfiction): Apex Books, 2017.

COLLECTIONS

Absent Company (fiction collection, ebook): Crossroad Press/Macabre Ink, 2014 (contents include *The Far Side of the Lake* collection, *Absences* collection, and *Among the Living*).

Celestial Inventories (fiction collection): ChiZine Publications, 2013.

City Fishing (fiction collection): Silver Salamander Press, 2000; (ebook): Crossroad Press/Macabre Ink, 2012.

Exploring Dark Short Fiction #1: A Primer to Steve Rasnic Tem (fiction collection, ed. Eric J. Guignard): Dark Moon Books, 2017.

The Far Side of the Lake (fiction collection): Ash-Tree Press, 2001 (contents also included in the ebook collection *Absent Company*).

Here With the Shadows (fiction collection): Swan River Press, 2014.

The Hydrocephalic Ward (poetry collection): Dark Regions Press, 2003.

In Concert (with Melanie Tem) (collection of collaborations): Centipede Press, 2010; (ebook): Crossroad Press, 2012.

Invisible (audio collection): read by Terry Daniel, Speaking Volumes, 2009.

Night Visions 1 (shared author fiction collection with Tanith Lee and Charles L. Grant, ed. Alan Ryan): Dark Harvest, 1984.

Ombres sur la Route (French language fiction collection): Denoel, 1994.

Onion Songs (fiction collection): Chomu Press, 2013.

Out of the Dark: A Storybook of Horrors (fiction collection): Centipede Press, 2016.

Twember: Science Fiction Stories; Imaginings vol. 7 (fiction collection):

NewCon Press, 2013.

Ugly Behavior (fiction collection): New Pulp Press, 2012.

ANTHOLOGIES AS EDITOR

High Fantastic: Colorado's Fantasy and Dark Fantasy: Ocean View Books, 1995.

The Umbral Anthology of Science Fiction Poetry: Umbral Press, 1982.

PLAYS

"A Hideous Idea"
    One-act dark suspense play, produced as part of *The Frankenstein Experiment*, Mary Miller Theatre, Lafayette, CO., Jan. 2006.

"The Mask Child: A Play for Puppets"
    (c) *Onion Songs* (f.c.): Chomu Press, 2013.

"Professor Potter's Lectures on Early Man (Decidedly NOT for Children)"
    A puppet play, *Imagination Box* CD, 2001.

GRAPHIC STORIES/ COMICS

"Cube" (graphic story; story and art)
    Slam Bang (comic anth., #2): Fan-Atic Press, 2006.

"Early Arrivals" (graphic story; story and art)
    Slam Bang (comic anth., #3): Fan-Atic Press, 2008.

"Shadowhouse" (graphic story; story and art)
    Blurred Vision: New Narrative Art (comic anth., #2–4): Blurred Books, 2006.

"Small Acts of Revenge" (graphic story; script only)

Death Rattle (comic anth., #18): Kitchen Sink Press, 1988.

"A Week During the Apocalypse" (graphic story; script only)
Negative Burn (comic anth., #49): Caliber Press, 1997.

ALSO FROM ERIC J. GUIGNARD AND DARK MOON BOOKS:

Every nation of the globe has unique tales to tell, whispers that settle in through the land, creatures or superstitions that enliven the night, but rarely do readers get to experience such a diversity of these voices in one place as in *A WORLD OF HORROR*, the latest anthology book created by award-winning editor Eric J. Guignard, and beautifully illustrated by artist Steve Lines.

Enclosed within its pages are twenty-two all-new dark and speculative fiction stories written by authors from around the world that explore the myths and monsters, fables and fears of their homelands.

Encounter the haunting things that stalk those radioactive forests outside Chernobyl in Ukraine; sample the curious dishes one may eat in Canada; beware the veldt monster that mirrors yourself in Uganda; or simply battle mountain trolls alongside Alfred Nobel in Sweden. These stories and more are found within *A World of Horror*: Enter and discover, truly, there's no place on the planet devoid of frights, thrills, and wondrous imagination.

"This breath of fresh air for horror readers shows the limitless possibilities of the genre."

—Publishers Weekly (starred review)

"A fresh collection of horror authors exploring monsters and myths from their homelands."

—Library Journal

Order your copy at www.darkmoonbooks.com or www.amazon.com
ISBN-13: 978-0-9989383-1-8

ALSO FROM ERIC J. GUIGNARD AND DARK MOON BOOKS:

Exploring Dark Short Fiction #2: A Primer to Kaaron Warren

Australian author Kaaron Warren is widely recognized as one of the leading writers today of speculative and dark short fiction. She's published four novels, multiple novellas, and well over one hundred heart-rending tales of horror, science fiction, and beautiful fantasy, and is the first author ever to simultaneously win all three of Australia's top speculative fiction writing awards (Ditmar, Shadows, and Aurealis awards for *The Grief Hole*).

Dark Moon Books and editor Eric J. Guignard bring you this introduction to her work, the second in a series of primers exploring modern masters of literary dark short fiction. Herein is a chance to discover—or learn more of—the distinct voice of Kaaron Warren, as beautifully illustrated by artist Michelle Prebich.

Included within these pages are:

- Six short stories, one written exclusively for this book
- Author interview
- Complete bibliography
- Academic commentary by Michael Arnzen, PhD (former humanities chair and professor of the year, Seton Hill University)
- ...and more!

Enter this doorway to the vast and fantastic: Get to know Kaaron Warren.

Order your copy at www.darkmoonbooks.com or www.amazon.com
ISBN-13: 978-0-9989383-0-1

ALSO FROM ERIC J. GUIGNARD AND DARK MOON BOOKS:

Exploring Dark Short Fiction #3: A Primer to Nisi Shawl

Praised by both literary journals and leading fiction magazines, Nisi Shawl is celebrated as an author whose works are lyrical and philosophical, speculative and far-ranging; "... broad in ambition and deep in accomplishment" (*The Seattle Times*). Besides nearly three decades of creating fantasy and science fiction stories, Nisi has also been lauded as editor, journalist, and proponent of feminism, African-American fiction, and other pedagogical issues of diversity.

Dark Moon Books and editor Eric J. Guignard bring you this introduction to her work, the third in a series of primers exploring modern masters of literary dark short fiction. Herein is a chance to discover—or learn more of—the vibrant voice of Nisi Shawl, as beautifully illustrated by artist Michelle Prebich.

Included within these pages are:

- Six short stories, one written exclusively for this book
- Author interview
- Complete bibliography
- Academic commentary by Michael Arnzen, PhD (former humanities chair and professor of the year, Seton Hill University)
- ... and more!

Enter this doorway to the vast and fantastic: Get to know Nisi Shawl.

Order your copy at www.darkmoonbooks.com or www.amazon.com
ISBN-13: 978-0-9989383-4-9

ALSO FROM ERIC J. GUIGNARD AND DARK MOON BOOKS:

POP THE CLUTCH:
THRILLING TALES OF
ROCKABILLY, MONSTERS,
AND HOT ROD HORROR

Welcome to the cool side of the 1950s, where the fast cars and revved-up movie monsters peel out in the night. Where outlaw vixens and jukebox tramps square off with razorblades and lead pipes. Where rockers rock, cool cats strut, and hot rods roar. Where you howl to the moon as the tiki drums pound and the electric guitar shrieks and that spit-and-holler jamboree ain't gonna stop for a long, long time ... maybe never.

This is the '50s where ghost shows still travel the back roads of the south, and rockabilly has a hold on the nation's youth; where lucky hearts tell the tale, and maybe that fella in the Shriners' fez ain't so square after all. Where exist noir detectives of the supernatural, tattoo artists of another kind, Hollywood fix-it men, and a punk kid with grasshopper arms under his chain-studded jacket and an icy stare on his face.

This is the '50s of *Pop the Clutch: Thrilling Tales of Rockabilly, Monsters, and Hot Rod Horror*. This is your ticket to the dark side of American kitsch ... the fun and frightful side!

"A fitting tribute to the 1950s with this 18-story compendium of hot rods, rock 'n' roll, and creature features come to life."

—*Publishers Weekly*

ALSO FROM ERIC J. GUIGNARD AND DARK MOON BOOKS:

Hearing, sight, touch, smell, and taste: Our impressions of the world are formed by our five senses, and so too are our fears, our imaginations, and our captivation in reading fiction stories that embrace these senses.

Whether hearing the song of infernal caverns, tasting the erotic kiss of treachery, or smelling the lush fragrance of a fiend, enclosed within this anthology are fifteen horror and dark fantasy tales that will quicken the beat of fear, sweeten the flavor of wonder, sharpen the spike of thrills, and otherwise brighten the marvel of storytelling that is found resonant!

Editor Eric J. Guignard and psychologist Jessica Bayliss, PhD also include companion discourse throughout, offering academic and literary insight as well as psychological commentary examining the physiology of our senses, why each of our senses are engaged by dark fiction stories, and how it all inspires writers to continually churn out ideas in uncommon and invigorating ways.

Featuring stunning interior illustrations by Nils Bross, and including fiction short stories by such world-renowned authors as John Farris, Ramsey Campbell, Poppy Z. Brite, Darrell Schweitzer, and Richard Christian Matheson, amongst others.

Intended for readers, writers, and students alike, explore *THE FIVE SENSES OF HORROR*!

Order your copy at www.darkmoonbooks.com or www.amazon.com
ISBN-13: 978-0-9988275-0-6

ALSO FROM ERIC J. GUIGNARD AND DARK MOON BOOKS:

Death. Who has not considered their own mortality and wondered at what awaits, once our frail human shell expires? What occurs after the heart stops beating, after the last breath is drawn, after life as we know it terminates?

Does our spirit remain on Earth while the body rots? Do the remnants of our soul transcend to a celestial Heaven or sink to Hell's torment? Can we choose our own afterlife? Can we die again in the hereafter? Are we given the opportunity to reincarnate and do it all over? Is life merely a cosmic joke or is it an experiment for something greater? Enclosed in this Bram Stoker-award winning anthology are thirty-four all-new dark and speculative fiction stories exploring the possibilities *AFTER DEATH . . .*

"Though the majority of the pieces come from the darker side of the genre, a solid minority are playful, clever, or full of wonder. This strong and well-themed anthology is sure to make readers contemplative even while it creates nightmares."

—Publishers Weekly

"In Eric J. Guignard's latest anthology he gathers some of the biggest and most talented authors on the planet to give us their take on this entertaining and perplexing subject matter . . . highly recommended."

—Famous Monsters of Filmland

"An excellent collection of imaginative tales of what waits beyond the veil."

—Amazing Stories Magazine

Order your copy at www.darkmoonbooks.com or www.amazon.com
ISBN-13: 978-0-9885569-2-8

ALSO FROM ERIC J. GUIGNARD AND DARK MOON BOOKS:

In this anthology, *DARK TALES OF LOST CIVILIZATIONS*, you will unearth twenty-five previously unpublished horror and speculative fiction stories relating to aspects of civilizations that are crumbling, forgotten, rediscovered, or perhaps merely spoken about in great and fearful whispers.

What is it that lures explorers to distant lands where none have returned? Where is Genghis Khan buried? What happened to Atlantis? Who will displace mankind on Earth? What laments have the Witches of Oz? Answers to these mysteries and other tales are presented within this critically acclaimed anthology.

"The stories range from mildly disturbing to downright terrifying… Most are written in a conservative, suggestive style, relying on the reader's own imagination to take the plunge from speculation to horror."

—*Monster Librarian Reviews*

"Several of these stories made it on to my best of the year shortlist, and the book itself is now on the best anthologies of the year shortlist."

—*British Fantasy Society*

"Almost any story in this anthology is worth the price of purchase. The entire collection is a delight."

—*Black Gate Magazine*

Order your copy at www.darkmoonbooks.com or www.amazon.com
ISBN-13: 978-0-9834335-9-0

ABOUT EDITOR,
ERIC J. GUIGNARD

ERIC J. GUIGNARD IS A writer and editor of dark and speculative fiction, operating from the shadowy outskirts of Los Angeles, where he also runs the small press Dark Moon Books. He's twice won the Bram Stoker Award (the highest literary award of horror fiction), been a finalist for the International Thriller Writers Award, and a multi-nominee of the Pushcart Prize.

He has over one hundred stories and non-fiction author credits appearing in publications around the world. As editor, Eric's published multiple fiction anthologies, including his most recent, *Pop the Clutch: Thrilling Tales of Rockabilly, Monsters, and Hot Rod Horror*; and *A World of Horror*, a showcase of international horror short fiction.

He currently publishes the acclaimed series of author primers created to champion modern masters of the dark and macabre, *Exploring Dark Short Fiction*. He is also publisher and acquisitions editor for the renowned *+Horror Library+* anthology series. Additionally he curates the series, *The Horror Writers Association Presents: Haunted Library of Horror Classics* through SourceBooks with co-editor Leslie S. Klinger.

His latest books are *Last Case at a Baggage Auction*; *Doorways To The Deadeye*; and short story collection *That Which Grows Wild: 16 Tales of Dark Fiction* (Cemetery Dance).

Outside the glamorous and jet-setting world of indie fiction, Eric's a technical writer and college professor, and he stumbles home each day to a wife, children, dogs, and a terrarium filled with mischievous beetles. Visit Eric at: www.ericjguignard.com, his blog: ericjguignard.blogspot.com, or Twitter: @ericjguignard.

ABOUT ACADEMIC, MICHAEL ARNZEN, PHD

MICHAEL A. ARNZEN (PhD, University of Oregon, 1999) teaches full-time at Seton Hill University, home of the country's only MFA degree in Writing Popular Fiction. To date he has won four Bram Stoker Awards and an International Horror Critics Guild Award for his often funny, always disturbing horror fiction and poetry, which  includes such book-length titles as *Grave Markings, Play Dead, Freakcidents,* and *Proverbs for Monsters.* Alongside Heidi Ruby Miller, Arnzen also co-edited *Many Genres, One Craft: Lessons in Writing Popular Fiction*—a large how-to guide for authors of speculative fiction and other genres. Arnzen continues to write horror and criticism while teaching the zombie populations near Pittsburgh, PA.

Follow Mike at https://gorelets.com and subscribe to his recently rebooted creative missive, *The Goreletter.* On top of his genre writing, Arnzen sits on the editorial board for *Paradoxa: Studies in World Literary Genres,* and his academic criticism has appeared in such journals as *Narrative, The Journal of Popular Film and Television,* and the *Journal of the Fantastic in the Arts.* He is developing an updated version of his doctoral dissertation, a critical survey of Freud's "unheimlich" in pop culture, called *The Popular Uncanny.*

ABOUT ILLUSTRATOR, MICHELLE PREBICH

MICHELLE PREBICH IS A freelance artist who studied Film Production, Theatre, and Fine Art at Cal-State Long Beach. A film and literature geek, she loves the dark/romantic era and existential themes.

She has worked as a production designer, artist, set dresser, property master, and special effects makeup artist on  short films, television segments, and web series for the film industry. Her collaboration with the band *Mr. Moonshine* includes art for their album and direction/design on two stop motion animation music videos. Her art he has been featured in galleries including Melt Down Comics and The Mystic Museum.

She sells original macabre art, art pieces, and apparel she has created through her shop "Bat in Your Belfry," which can be found at batinyourbelfry.etsy.com and on Instagram @batinyourbelfry. She loves geeking out with fellow enthusiasts of the unusual and macabre and can be typically found at Halloween/horror conventions usually standing next to a man in a cowboy hat.

About the Author

Claire Boston is a contemporary romance author who enjoys exploring real life issues on her way to the happily-ever-after. She writes heart-warming stories, with resilient heroines and heroes you'll love. In 2014 she was nominated for an Australian Romance Readers Award for Favourite New Romance Author.

When Claire's not writing she can be found creating her own handmade journals, swinging on a sidecar, or in the garden attempting to grow something other than weeds.

Claire lives in Western Australia with her husband, who loves even her most annoying quirks, and her grubby, but adorable Australian bulldog.

You can connect with Claire through Facebook (https://www.facebook.com/clairebostonauthor) and Twitter (https://www.twitter.com/clairebauthor), or join her reader group (http://www.claireboston.com/reader-group/).

Also by Claire Boston